"They're coming W9-CRG-590

"Hold on!" Tucker sped up and maneuvered into the right lane, dodging around another car.

The truck copied his moves and accelerated into the left lane beside them. Their window opened and a rifle appeared.

"Gun!" Madison yelled.

Tucker hit the brakes, and the cruiser's tires screeched. The vehicle swerved as he fought to maintain control.

Madison pointed to an upcoming exit. "Take that road! We need to get off the busy highway and not endanger lives."

Tucker sped up, and at the last minute he steered onto the ramp, catching the assailants off guard. The F-150 missed the exit and raced down the road. Tucker radioed his fellow officers, giving them the vehicle's description and where the truck was last seen.

Madison exhaled. "Close call. What do you think they wanted?"

"You."

"What? Why?"

"You became a target as soon as you found that thumb drive. I'm guessing the people in the truck were the same ones who fired on us earlier. They're watching us."

Darlene L. Turner is an award-winning author who lives with her husband, Jeff, in Ontario, Canada. Her love of suspense began when she read her first Nancy Drew book. She's turned that passion into her writing and believes readers will be captured by her plots, inspired by her strong characters and moved by her inspirational message. Visit Darlene at www.darlenelturner.com, where there's suspense beyond borders.

Books by Darlene L. Turner

Love Inspired Suspense

Border Breach
Abducted in Alaska
Lethal Cover-Up

Visit the Author Profile page at Harlequin.com.

LETHAL COVER-UP

DARLENE L. TURNER

LOVE INSPIRED SUSPENSE
INSPIRATIONAL ROMANCE

If you purchased this book without a cover you should be aware
that this book is stolen property. It was reported as "unsold and
destroyed" to the publisher, and neither the author nor the
publisher has received any payment for this "stripped book."

LOVE INSPIRED® SUSPENSE
INSPIRATIONAL ROMANCE

ISBN-13: 978-1-335-72255-3

Lethal Cover-Up

Copyright © 2021 by Darlene L. Turner

All rights reserved. No part of this book may be used or reproduced in
any manner whatsoever without written permission except in the case of
brief quotations embodied in critical articles and reviews.

This is a work of fiction. Names, characters, places and incidents are either the
product of the author's imagination or are used fictitiously. Any resemblance
to actual persons, living or dead, businesses, companies, events or locales is
entirely coincidental.

This edition published by arrangement with Harlequin Books S.A.

For questions and comments about the quality of this book, please contact us
at CustomerService@Harlequin.com.

Love Inspired
22 Adelaide St. West, 40th Floor
Toronto, Ontario M5H 4E3, Canada
www.Harlequin.com

Printed in U.S.A.

Recycling programs
for this product may
not exist in your area.

PLEASE RECYCLE
THIS PRODUCT IS RECYCLABLE

Be of good courage, and he shall strengthen your heart,
all ye that hope in the Lord.
—*Psalm* 31:24

For Susan, my beautiful sister and cheerleader

ONE

"They're after me!"

Border patrol officer Madison Steele stiffened at the sound of her sister's frantic voice and gripped her cell phone tighter. A tremor snaked up her spine. She'd just found the sister she never knew about, and now she was in danger? Madison turned her booth's light to red and stepped outside the Canada Border Services Agency at the New Brunswick–Maine border. Thankfully, the early rush-hour traffic had ended, allowing her time to take her sister's call.

"Slow down, Leah. Who's after you? What are you talking about?" The crisp fall noon air nipped at her and she pulled her vest tighter.

"My employer. I have incriminating evidence against them. Now they want me out of the way." Leah's words came out breathless. "They're shipping nonsanctioned over-the-counter drugs across your border."

What? Madison took pride in her job, stopping illegal shipments from creeping into Canada. How were they getting the goods past the CBSA? Her mind flooded with unanswered questions. Did her boss know?

Tires screeching on pavement sailed through Madison's cell phone. "Leah! Are you okay?"

"They're gaining on me."

"Where are you?" Madison couldn't lose Leah. Not now. Not after all their lost years. Madison had discovered at age seventeen she was adopted. Her parents had kept it a secret, and she only found out through the mean, popular girls in high school. They had told her she'd never make prom queen because no one liked her. "Not even your real parents," they had said. One of their mothers found out about Madison's adoption through her local sorority-sister events. Gossip spreads quickly in a small town. Madison had confronted her mom and dad when she got home. They didn't deny it. That was the night Madison lost trust and hope in God.

"Hawthorne Street. Heading your way."

Leah's directions snapped Madison back to the present.

"Sissy, you have to see what's happening at Dolumhart Pharmaceuticals. Tainted—"

Metal-upon-metal scraping boomed in Madison's ear. "Leah!" Every muscle froze, immobilizing her in place.

A muffled scream thundered through the phone as a crunch sounded, followed by silence.

"No!" Madison sprang into action. She called 911 relaying her sister's location and raced toward the border station, abandoning her booth. She opened the door and collided with her superintendent. "I need to leave. My sister. Car accident." Her scrambled words matched her pounding heartbeat.

"Go!" Superintendent Sam Watson handed her keys. "Take my cruiser."

"Thank you." She ran to the vehicle and hopped in as her memory flashed to the first meeting with Leah. The petite brunette had beamed from ear to ear, not only smiling with her lips, but her button brown eyes. They connected instantly and their bond grew into a solid friendship. The fact that Madison finally had the older sister she'd always wanted had warmed her heart. What would she do if that unexpected gift was ripped away?

No, she wouldn't go there. She white-knuckled the wheel and pulled onto the highway toward Hawthorne Street, flicking on the flashing lights and siren. She couldn't waste precious time.

Minutes later, she sped around a sharp turn and gasped at the sight along the street. "No!"

Police, firefighters and an ambulance had beaten her to the scene. Leah's green SUV was entwined around an enormous Norway maple tree, smoke rising from it. The front end obliterated.

Lord, no! Help Leah to be okay.

Wait? Had she just prayed to God, who she'd abandoned? She tightened her hands on the wheel. No, she wouldn't concede to someone who allowed such pain in her life.

Madison shook off thoughts of God and jerked the cruiser to the side of the road. She jumped out and raced to her sister as flames shot out from under the smashed hood. "Leah!"

A slender police constable pulled her back. "Miss, stay here. Let the firefighters do their job."

She yanked her arm free. "That's my sister!" Madison knew she was being unprofessional, but she didn't care. She ran closer to the vehicle.

A bulky firefighter stood in her path, holding his hands in a stop position. "Whoa! You can't go any farther."

"Ma'am. What's your sister's name?" The officer came up behind her.

"Leah Peters," Madison said with a shaky voice.

He wrote it down and fished out his cell phone as he stepped away.

Another firefighter extinguished the fire. Steam billowed upward, creating a haze against the blue sky. "We need the hydraulic cutters!" he yelled from his position.

The others rushed forward with the Jaws of Life and pried open Leah's door. They hauled her from the wreckage as the two paramedics moved in. The female placed her fingers on Leah's neck, checking for a pulse.

Madison held her breath.

Moments snuck by but seemed like an eternity.

"No pulse." The female settled her cheek near Leah's mouth and watched her chest. The woman popped her head up. "She's not breathing. Hook up an EKG lead." She pulled Leah's clothing away.

The other paramedic attached the machine.

"Come on, Leah. Come back to me." Madison's

whispered plea faded into the flatlined tone of the machine.

The male hung his head. "Call the coroner."

"Please, God, no!" Madison pushed forward to Leah and dropped. She wrapped her arms around her sister's lifeless body, placed her head on Leah's chest, and sobbed. She sensed the paramedics and firefighters moved away, allowing her time to say goodbye when she'd just said hello to her half sister. They'd only found each other six months ago. How could she lose her now?

She raised herself into a seated position. "I promise I will not rest until I find who did this to you." A promise she vowed not to break. Tears streamed down Madison's cheeks. "I will never forget you, Sissy." Their term of endearment. She kissed Leah's forehead.

"Preliminary findings reveal she lost control going around the curve too fast," one police officer said in hushed tones close to where Madison mourned.

She jumped to her feet, heat flushing her cheeks. "This was not an accident!"

The man stepped closer to her, pen and notebook in hand. "Why would you say that? Nothing here points to foul play."

How did he know that so fast? Suspicion reared its head like an ugly, fast-growing weed, overpowering her thoughts. Was this cop dirty? She'd heard rumors of officers being bought lately by organized crime members. One officer had been incarcerated with the heroin smuggling plot she'd uncovered a few months ago. Were there more swayed by the promise of unending riches?

She shrugged off the thoughts and concentrated on her sister's case. "Leah called me from her car. She was on her way to see me at the CBSA station. Someone was chasing her."

"I'm Constable Jenkins," the officer said. "You are?"

"Madison Steele."

"What did your sister tell you?"

She hesitated. How much should she share? She had to put faith in these men. They were her fellow law enforcement community. "That they were after her because she had incriminating evidence against Dolumhart Pharmaceuticals."

The man's glance darted back to Leah's car. Was that a look of panic flashing across his face? Why?

Another tremor of suspicion scrambled through her body, but she suppressed her mistrust for now. "Call in your Major Crimes Unit. They need to investigate—"

An unmarked cruiser screeched around the corner with its lights flashing and parked along the road.

"Seems like someone else has done just that," Constable Jenkins said. "There he is now."

A man stepped from the vehicle and glanced in their direction.

Madison squinted. Was that—?

It had been years since she'd seen his handsome face, but she'd know him anywhere.

The boy whose heart she'd shattered on prom night walked toward them.

"Tucker?"

Canadian police constable Tucker Reed halted midstep at the sight of the woman before him. Her blue eyes thrust him back to his high school prom night. Eyes that had held disgust after he'd announced his new faith in Christ. At the end of the evening, she ripped away the future he thought they had. Why was she here?

Tucker had recently returned to his hometown after being tasked to the local police detachment as a liaison for the Major Crimes Unit in Saint John. He'd been called to the scene of the accident by a powerful man. One who wanted answers.

"Madi?" He noticed her border-patrol uniform. He hadn't heard she'd joined the CBSA.

She flinched at the sound of the nickname he'd given her when they became friends and then sweethearts. "No one calls me that anymore." She bit her lip and crossed her arms.

"Sorry. Why are you here?"

Tears filled her eyes. "My sister just died in this accident."

Wait. Madi was an only child. "Leah Peters was your sister?"

She nodded. "We just found each other."

Jenkins drew his notebook from his pocket. "Constable Reed, who called you here?"

"Emerson Peters."

The officer sucked in a breath. "Why would the politician call the MCU and how did he find out about the accident so quickly?"

"We're friends and he wanted someone he knew in the area to investigate his daughter's accident. Her vehicle's automatic collision notification system sent the accident data to her insurance company upon impact. It's a feature on her car. They called him because she had listed her father as a contact on her policy."

Madi's lips curled as a flash of anger skirted over her pretty face. "Why isn't he here?"

"He's on his way back from Ottawa but doesn't know of Leah's death yet." Why did Madi hold contempt toward the politician? Tucker became friends with Emerson when they'd met in Saint John at a law enforcement meeting a year ago. The politician was raising support to run for his party leadership, hoping to become New Brunswick's next premier, and wanted to get the police force on board. He'd promised them he'd do everything in his power to get additional funding to police departments. Tucker suspected his promotion to the MCU had come at Emerson's request, or at least a hand in it.

"Well, all evidence so far suggests this was an

accident." Constable Jenkins pointed at the road. "Look at those skids."

Darkened tire marks curved before their impact with the tree. Other officers placed evidence markers at various points on the pavement as golden, red and orange leaves swirled from nearby trees, settling among the police indicators.

Paramedics covered Leah with a tarp, and the female officer spoke into her cell phone. They would call in the coroner to attend to the body. His job was to determine whether it was an accident. Well, not normally a job for his unit, but Emerson was insistent Corporal Hyatt task Tucker to the case.

The other paramedic attended to a firefighter's hand.

Tucker turned back to his fellow officer. "Hyatt has put me in charge of this investigation at Emerson Peters's request. All evidence is to go through me. Understood?" He didn't want to pull rank, but he realized this case would soon be elevated once the press caught wind of the high-profile victim.

Constable Jenkins scowled. "Fine." He ripped a page from his notebook and thrust it into Tucker's hand. "Here. Everything I have. Which isn't much." He stomped over to the onsite collision analyst and reconstructionist's team.

Tucker pulled out his cell phone. "Madison, I need to call Mr. Peters. I'll be right back."

He stepped away and hit the man's number. He hated to do this over the phone but had no choice.

"Tucker, what's going on?" The politician's shaky voice held concern.

"Sir, I realize you're on your way back home and I would rather tell you this news in person, but I wanted to advise you before the press is alerted. I'm so sorry. Leah died at the accident scene."

The normally composed man sobbed on the other end of the phone. "What happened?" His question came out breathless.

"It appears like she raced around the curve and hit a tree."

Emerson cursed. "That's not how my daughter drives. Something doesn't sound right here."

"What do you mean?"

"She told me recently she'd discovered some cover-ups at work and was concerned for her safety. Tucker, this was no accident. Find my daughter's murderer."

"Corporal Hyatt put me in charge. I will leave no stone unturned. I promise."

"Good. I'm counting on you." He clicked off.

No pressure. Emerson Peters was one person Tucker didn't want to cross. He had friends in high places and was known for being ruthless.

Tucker pocketed his phone and walked back to where Madi stood.

She fisted her hands, placing them on her hips. "Leah was murdered."

Not her too. "Why do you think that?"

Her tortured expression flashed wrenching pain.

"She called me moments before her accident and told me she had incriminating evidence against her employer, Dolumhart Pharmaceuticals. She used the word tainted before I heard the crash and the call dropped. She—"

Madi looked away, but not before he saw her eyes moisten.

"I'm so sorry for your loss."

Another officer approached and stood in front of her. "You Madison Steele?"

"Yes."

He handed her an envelope. "We found this in the glove box with your name on it."

"Wait!" Tucker pulled gloves from his back pocket. "Put these on, Madi."

She scowled.

"Sorry. Madison." Why did he divert to using her nickname after so many years?

She put on the gloves, opened the envelope and read. A tear escaped, but she swatted it away and shoved the note to him, determination etched on her face. "I need to examine my sister's vehicle."

He read the note.

Sissy, if you're reading this, I'm probably dead. They found out I stole evidence. I put it in my car in a place you once told me people hide things to smuggle across borders. Please find it and bring these criminals to justice. I love you. Come back to God. He loves you too. Remember, #SistersForever.

2I&B,
Leah xo

He held the note out to the officer. "Bag this as evidence." He turned to Madi. "The officers will examine the car."

She tapped her toe and folded her arms across her chest. "Tucker, tearing cars apart is a daily occurrence for a border patrol officer. I need access to her vehicle."

"Where do you think she hid it?"

Madi adjusted her long blonde braid, pushing it to one side. "I told her a number of places, so I'm not positive which one she would have chosen."

"Tell us and we'll look."

She clutched his arm. "You have to let me do this. She was my sister."

"Fine. What tools do you need?"

"There should be some in my superintendent's SUV." She raced over to the CBSA vehicle and pulled out a bag from the rear.

The autumn winds swept in and scooped up Madi's braid, thrusting it back and forth. Her small frame swayed as she headed toward him. Not much had changed in the last ten years. She still had her adorable childlike face.

Not that he was looking.

She held up the bag. "Let's do this."

Tucker requested the other constables step back to allow Officer Steele to do her examination of her sister's car. The one paramedic continued treatment on the firefighter's hands as the other moved their equipment back into the ambulance.

Madi worked quickly around the vehicle, tapping on the tires before moving to the bumpers and inspecting all the cracks. Next, she removed the side door panels and searched inside each one.

Nothing.

He observed Madi as she examined the seats, looking under and feeling around the crevices. She stood and wiped her forehead with the back of her gloved hand, confusion written on her face.

Would her sister have misled Madi? "Have you looked everywhere you told her?"

She twirled the end of her braid as if that helped her think. Seconds later, her steely blue eyes widened and she held up a finger. "One place I haven't checked." She sat back inside the car.

Tucker moved into the passenger seat. "Where are you thinking?"

"Air vents would be a good place to hide something like a flash drive, especially since it's not hot enough for air conditioning and not cold enough for defrosting. She probably had to make a quick decision on where to put it. However, with the damage done to the front end, I'm not sure anything would be salvaged." Madi moved her fingers around the dented vents and stopped. "There's something there, but it's stuck. Hand me the screwdriver from the bag."

Tucker rummaged through and found it, then gave it to her.

She poked it into the blocked vent and pushed it to the left.

An object flew out and landed in her lap. She held it up.

A thumb drive.

"Well done, Officer Steele." Tucker was impressed with her thoroughness.

Her lips quivered. "My sister died to protect this. I need to find out what's on it."

"We have to do this the right way. We'll bag it and take it to the station." Even if he knew she'd want to be involved, he prided himself on logging evidence correctly. Especially after the rookie mistakes he'd made in his early years when he failed to ask questions and thought he could do everything on his own only to find out his reports were incorrect and sloppy. Plus, he had missed valuable intel by not paying attention to vital details. He promised himself he'd never fall into that trap again.

They got out of the car and Tucker waved another constable over. "We need an evidence bag."

The older officer approached. "What did you find?"

Madi held up the flash drive. "What happens now?"

"We'll dust for fingerprints to ensure it only has Leah's on it. Then—"

Bullets slammed into the SUV.

Multiple gunshots boomed.

"Get down!" Tucker grabbed Madi and shoved her behind the ambulance.

He unleashed his 9 mm and peeked around the vehicle.

Another round from the opposite direction peppered the area.

They were pinned down.

TWO

Tucker pulled out his radio. "Jenkins, can you see the shooter from your vantage point?" They needed to contain the situation before someone else got hurt. This attack proved one thing. Madi was right. This was no accident. However, they'd send the vehicle for analysis to be one-hundred-percent certain, but his gut told him they targeted Leah. How long had the assailants been watching them?

"No, but there's definitely more than one," Jenkins said. "Hyatt is en route."

"Copy that." Tucker pocketed the radio and peeked around the ambulance, pointing his weapon in different directions. The noonday sun blinded him from catching any movement in the area. Were the assailants gone?

Madi slid to the ground, holding her head.

"What's wrong?" Tucker holstered his gun and knelt beside her.

She held her fingertips on top of a gash above her eye. "Hit my head on the side of the ambulance when you shoved me behind it. Didn't think much of it, but suddenly it started pounding."

"Sorry for pushing so hard, but I had to get you out of the way." He stood. "I'll get a paramedic."

Sirens exploded onto the scene.

Seconds later, the shots ceased.

His corporal pulled up beside them and got out,

crouching low with his weapon raised. "Reed, you okay?"

"Yes, but Madison needs a paramedic." Tucker helped Madi to her feet. "Corporal Greg Hyatt, have you met CBSA Officer Madison Steele in your travels? The victim was her sister."

Madi nodded. "Nice to see you again, Corporal."

"So sorry for your loss. You've got quite the gouge there." Hyatt's radio crackled. "Go ahead."

"Perimeter secure, sir. Scoured the area. No sign of the assailants." Jenkins's winded words sounded jagged. "Reed, scene is all yours." His sarcastic comment held disdain.

Tucker had only worked with the team for two months, but for some reason Jenkins had it in for him. He argued with almost every decision and report Tucker filed. Plus, Hyatt seemed to favor the tall constable over the rest of the team. Tucker struggled with proving himself capable, so hopefully solving this case would help and show him worthy to be in their unit.

"Good job, Jenkins." Hyatt banged the side of the ambulance. "Shooters are gone. Need a paramedic over here."

Moments later, a tall raven-haired woman appeared with her bag. "Who needs help?"

Tucker stepped forward. "Charlotte Dixon? From St. Stephen High?"

She squinted and put her hands on her hips.

"Well, I'll be. Tucker Reed. When did you get back in town?"

"Couple months ago."

"Surprised I haven't seen you around." She sized him up. "You haven't changed a bit. Still the handsome guy I remember."

Really? Did she just hit on him at a crime scene? She hadn't changed either. Still the same flirt. "Charlotte, you remember Madison Steele, right? She's hurt."

The woman's dark brown eyes narrowed. "Of course. We've seen each other around town. I didn't realize it was you earlier. I was focused on the victim." She put on her gloves. "Let me check." She stepped closer and removed Madi's hand, then pressed on the wound.

Madi winced. "Easy, Charlotte."

The paramedic dressed and bandaged the cut. "You're all set." Charlotte's radio sounded, announcing another call. "Gotta run. See you around, Tucker." She winked.

He suppressed a sigh. "Thanks for your help." She was one childhood classmate he'd hoped to avoid. Tucker despised catty women, and she had always fit that bill.

The coroner's vehicle pulled up beside the wreckage and an older gentleman stepped out. He adjusted his bow tie and sauntered over to Leah's covered body.

Tucker caught Madi's expression when she

watched the man remove the tarp. Tears welled, and she bit her lower lip. Obviously trying to stop herself from losing control in front of everyone. He needed to get her to their detachment and check out the flash drive. Anything to remove her from this tragic scene.

He turned to Hyatt. "You okay if I take Madison to the station and look at the flash drive? My guess is whoever was shooting at us wanted it. We need to see what's on it and Leah was Madison's sister. She could help."

The older officer removed his hat and scratched his head. "She's law enforcement and has a trained eye. Sure. You go. We'll continue to investigate this scene. Jenkins will impound the car for inspection."

"Something tells me they'll find some type of tampering," Tucker said.

"Well, until we're sure, I'm still calling this an accident." Hyatt took a step but turned. "Even if the victim's father is an esteemed politician."

Was that a jab at Tucker for being friends with Emerson? He knew the corporal resisted Tucker's promotion to the MCU and placed within their station, but why take it out on him? In the short time Tucker had been home, he'd already proven his capabilities in solving an old cold case. Or at least he thought he'd shown his worth. He rubbed his brow and walked back to Madi.

"You and I are going to the station. Are you able to get away from your shift to help me check the drive? Since you knew Leah best, I think you could help."

She removed her cell phone from her pocket. "I'll check with Superintendent Watson."

Fifteen minutes later, Tucker sat at his desk and inserted the flash drive.

Madi received permission from her boss to help the police for the day. She dragged a chair beside him and sat.

Her familiar lavender scent wafted around his work station, taking him back to their teenage romance and the night she'd shattered his heart. He still didn't know the real reason she'd broken it off. She had refused to see him after that and wouldn't take his calls. Even unfriended him on social media.

He breathed in and exhaled.

"What?"

Caught in his youthful reminiscence. "I've missed your lavender." Half-truth. Who was he kidding? Seeing her again slammed his feelings back similar to an old movie rewinding at full speed. He needed to curb whatever emotion had sparked, especially after finding out the news of his father's genetic Huntington's Disease condition. After his father's death, his mother admitted to this being the reason his father left them many years ago. Tucker would not give his heart to a woman knowing he may have the gene. His mother pleaded with him to get tested, but Tucker didn't want to know. The unknown was too scary.

"Let's check the drive, shall we?" Madi's tense voice brought him back to the task at hand.

"Right." Enough of memories and what-ifs. He clicked the drive. A password box displayed. Great. "Any ideas what she would've used? If not, we'll get forensics involved." They would anyway, but Tucker wanted a first glance at whatever Leah had documented.

Madi tapped her index finger on her chin. "Um. Try her birth day and month. 0728."

He typed it in. Access denied dinged at them. "Nope."

"Try spelling out the month."

Access denied.

"Think. If we try too many combinations, we may get locked out if she put a fail-safe on it."

"Try #SistersForever," Madi said.

He eyed her. "I saw this on Leah's note. What does it mean?"

"A hashtag we liked to use."

"When did you find each other?"

"Six months ago." She bit her lip and gazed out the window. "She was ripped away too soon."

He squeezed her hand. "I'm sorry, Madi."

"Stop calling me that." She snapped her hand back and shoved it into her pocket.

He bristled. *Too soon, Tucker.* He turned back to the computer and typed in the sister code.

A slew of folders, videos, and photos popped on his screen.

Madi sat forward, her eyes bulging.

"Whoa. Looks like she's been collecting evidence for a while. Some of these date back three months ago." Tucker clicked the oldest folder.

"Why didn't she tell me before today?" Her voice quivered. "I could've helped."

"She probably wanted to be sure." The folder expanded and revealed multiple Word documents. He opened one.

Test results for a new over-the-counter drug called Morvecet appeared on his screen and he read through the findings.

Drug has caused symptoms including hives, extreme migraines, dizziness, muscle tension and sometimes...

Death.

What? Tucker's mother took this drug for chronic back pain.

Fear spiked his body, pulsating through his nervous system. He bolted from his chair.

He'd lost one parent and couldn't lose another.

Madison jerked backward in her chair at Tucker's sudden movement. What had him riled? She leaned forward and read her sister's documentation. The findings revealed upsetting stats on how many adverse reactions the volunteer patients from the Morvecet clinical trials had reported. Even death.

Why had this caused Tucker's response? She stood and faced him. "What's wrong?"

He ran his fingers through his wavy dark brown hair. "My mother is on that drug."

"How did she get it?"

"Not sure, but I will find out," Tucker said.

She grabbed his arm. "She'll be okay. Tell her to slowly wean off of it until we find out more."

His gorgeous cornflower blue eyes widened.

She remembered how close he and his mother were, especially after his father had left them for no apparent reason. "Call Bev. Now."

He nodded and walked into the hall, pulling out his cell phone.

Madison moved back to Tucker's laptop and continued to read through the drug reactions. The amount of volunteers in the clinical trials numbered in the hundreds, so after these conclusions why hadn't they stopped the production process?

Or were they hiding the results?

Could that be why Leah had called her this morning in a frantic state?

Madison opened a video file.

The back of a man's head appeared in a darkened room. The shot's strange angle piqued Madison's curiosity. She pressed Play.

"What do you mean it kills?" the raspy, distorted voice asked.

"Reports reveal adverse reactions including death. We need to stop producing the drug. The

FDA and HPFB are both coming down hard on us after complaints." The other man was off camera, but his high-pitched voice personified his panicked state. "We'll be sued."

"We can't stop now. Doctor the results."

"She knows."

"We bury her reports and…"

The voice trailed off, and the camera bounced as if the person taping it was trying to get closer.

Was it her sister? Madison held her breath.

"Are you prepared to make that sacrifice?" the grating voice asked. "We have too much at stake."

"Don't you threaten me. Remember who's in charge here."

There was a muffled noise in the background.

The man turned slightly, but not enough to see his face. "What was that?"

The video ended.

Did they catch her sister recording their conversation? And who was talking? The voices were distorted.

Madison buried her head in her hands. *What did you do, Sissy? Why didn't you call me sooner?*

Grief flooded every ounce of her as tremors threatened to incapacitate her. She felt a gentle hand on her shoulder.

"Madi, what is it?"

For once, his term of endearment didn't irritate her. She glanced up at her childhood sweetheart, who'd grown into a handsome man. Why had she broken up with him again?

Right. He'd become a Christian, and she knew she could never give her heart to someone who trusted in an unseen entity. Not after all the pain she'd gone through. Especially if he'd known how she had graffitied several churches in a rebellious rage against God when she was a teenager.

She moved back into her chair, ignoring what his touch did to her. "Watch this video."

He sat and pressed Play.

Madison leaned in to get a better audio on the voices, but it was too difficult. The poor state inhibited the video quality.

"One voice sounds oddly familiar to me, but I'm not sure from where." Tucker played it again but shook his head. "Nope, can't place it. It's too distorted and you can barely hear their conversation. I'm going to send it to forensics. Maybe they can clean it up." He typed on his keyboard and pressed Enter. "Done."

"Leah stumbled onto a major drug cover-up and paid the price for it." Madison's voice exposed both her grief and anger, but she straightened. Resolved to uncover whoever did this to the sister she'd just found. For now, she needed to change the subject. "How's Bev?"

"Resting. She promised she'd decrease her dosage and stop the drug in a few days. Let's pray her condition improves."

Pray? That wouldn't help.

Madison set the thought aside and eyed the remainder of the files. She pointed to one. "What's that?"

Tucker opened it.

An official letter from the Food and Drug Administration (FDA) and Health Products and Food Branch (HPFB) of Health Canada giving the company the go-ahead to move to the next clinical trial phase on Morvecet. It was dated three months ago. A document was embedded into the letter. He double clicked on it.

Test results from their first clinical trial popped up, but they didn't match the previous ones.

Madison bolted out of her chair, knocking it over. "They doctored the results!" She paced around his desk. "No wonder Leah wanted to bring her employer to justice. Dolumhart Pharmaceuticals lied." Madison pointed. "What's that?"

Tucker clicked on an Excel spreadsheet. Financials for the drug production appeared, listing the costs of the ingredients with a comparison of a cheaper substitute version for each. The differences were astronomical.

"Click the next tab," Madison said.

A list of actual ingredients they used displayed. They had chosen the less expensive and dangerous ones.

Madison fisted her hands. "They took shortcuts.

No wonder the drug had such adverse reactions. They didn't care. All they wanted was a quick buck."

Tucker huffed out a sigh. "The FDA and HPFB don't realize Dolumhart tainted the drug. And your sister collected evidence against the company, but did she confront the owners?"

"Let's keep going." She pointed to another file. "Open this one. Please."

A shipping manifest with all addresses redacted from the document.

"Click the financials again. I want to see how much they'd lose if they had told the truth about the drug."

Tucker toggled back to the spreadsheet.

Madison drew in a sharp breath. "No wonder they lied. They stood to lose millions."

"But it's not like Dolumhart couldn't afford the hit. Their yearly gross earnings top in the billions of dollars."

"Someone high in the company didn't want to take a pay cut. Let me see the shipping manifest again."

He clicked on it and pointed to an entry. "Last shipment was two days ago."

Madison sat and slouched back in her chair. "That's my border, and I was on shift that day." Her cheeks burned as thickness clogged her throat. How did they get it past her?

"But you wouldn't have even known about the illegal activity. You can't blame yourself."

She knew he was right, but why did she feel responsible for her sister's death?

Madison eyed another folder and pointed. "Click that."

He opened the file and a copy of an email popped up.

One from Leah Peters to the CEO of Dolumhart Pharmaceuticals, Brechin Cross, copying her vice president, Daniel Levine.

Dear Mr. Cross,

This email is to notify you that Dolumhart Pharmaceuticals falsified the Morvecet test results. I reported the adverse findings to the vice president of our New Brunswick division, but no one has heeded my advice. Therefore, I'm informing you that I plan to go to the press if you don't cease manufacturing this terrible drug. Lives are at stake.

Yours truly,
Leah Peters
Clinical Project Manager

Her sister's email was dated yesterday.

The day before her death.

Had Mr. Cross been the one to put a hit out on Leah? Or was it Daniel Levine?

She fisted her hands. They needed to find out fast. Before they lost other lives.

THREE

Tucker caught Madi's agitated expression on her contorted face. The timing of her sister's email and crash were no accident. Was the CEO responsible? Or had someone hacked Leah's account? In this day and age hackers ran rampant getting into user's emails, cell phones and banks. No one was safe. Not even law enforcement.

"I'm sorry, Madison. This is definitely looking suspicious and I'm sure once forensics inspects Leah's vehicle, they'll prove it was murder." Tucker closed the email. "I just have to convince Corporal Hyatt."

"What do you mean?" Madi asked.

"For some reason he has it in for me. Doesn't feel I got the position within MCU legitimately. That Emerson pushed my leader in Saint John to promote me."

"You're friends with Leah's father?" Her lips curled into a frown.

"You don't like the man?"

She shrugged. "I really don't know him."

Tucker's cell phone buzzed. He glanced at the caller. "Speaking of Hyatt." He stood and walked down the hall. "Corporal. You done at the scene? Anything new?"

"No. Just wrapping up. What did you find on the drive?"

Tucker shared the information they discovered. "We need to find out how this tainted drug is getting across the border and into the public's hands, so we can stop it. Can you set up a joint task force with the CBSA and get Madison involved?"

"Do you think that's wise? She's too close and should be excused. I was okay with her looking at the drive, but I'm not so sure she should be involved further."

Probably true, but Tucker remembered Madi's stubborn streak. She wouldn't let anyone else near the case. "I can vouch for her. She'll stay focused."

Corporal Hyatt huffed. "Peters will have my head if you two screw this up. I'm going to task Jenkins to your team to keep you accountable. He's looking into the SUV tampering but will join you tomorrow."

Figures. The man didn't trust Tucker. "Fine."

"I'll call Madison's boss. Stay tuned."

"In the meantime, I'll—"

Hyatt ended the call, cutting Tucker off.

Tucker shook his head and pocketed his phone, making his way back to Madi.

She was immersed in reviewing the documentation and rubbed her neck muscles.

Tucker sat and eyed the file she was reading. The shipping manifest. A question raced through his mind. Could she remain objective? He needed to know.

"Corporal Hyatt has agreed to a joint task force.

He's calling your boss now." He paused. "Madison, before we get started, I need to ask you a question."

"What?"

"Can you remain impartial in your sister's case?"

Her eyes flashed. "I realize we haven't seen each other for years, but do you really need to ask that?"

"Don't worry. I vouched for you, but I just need to be sure. She was your sister and I understand you want to catch those responsible, but we need to do everything by the book. To the letter."

She threw up her hands. "I get it and I will. I promise. I need to see this through."

"Understood." Tucker sent some documents to his email to be accessible on his cell phone. Next, he selected all the files and copied them to another USB drive before removing the disk. "Just in case. We'll drop the flash drive to forensics on the way."

"Where are we going?"

"Our first stop. Dolumhart Pharmaceuticals. I want to show them your sister's email and have a chat with the VP." He stood. "Oh, Jenkins will join the task force tomorrow."

Her cell phone buzzed and she swiped the screen. "My boss giving me authorization to join the team."

"Good. Let's go."

A few minutes later after dropping off the USB stick, Tucker turned onto the highway toward the pharmaceutical conglomerate's satellite office on the outskirts of St. Stephen. Their principal build-

ing was downtown Saint John—one hour from
their location.

"How long did Leah work for Dolumhart?"
Tucker asked.

"Fifteen years. She started in their head office
but was promoted two years ago to a Clinical Project Manager and moved back to St. Stephen. They
wanted someone close to the border to work with
their counterparts at the U.S. division."

"And closer to her father."

Madi pinched the bridge of her nose. "Yes. Some
say he got her the job."

Kind of like him. "I know the feeling. I didn't
realize you had a sister. Tell me about how you met
Leah. When did you find out about her?"

"Long story, but I'll give you the abridged version." Madi shifted in her seat. "Something I never
told you, but just before graduation, I found out I
was adopted."

"What?"

She glanced out the window, but not before he
caught the anger creep onto her pretty face.

"I had a hard time dealing with it," she continued. "I confronted my parents. They didn't deny
it. Two days later they were dead."

Madi's parents were wealthy. Her father was a
CEO of a bank and her mother a lawyer. Just before
graduation, they were killed in a plane crash. He
had tried to contact Madi after she broke up with

him, but she wouldn't see him. Shortly after that, he'd left for the university.

"Why didn't you tell me?"

She opened her window a crack. "I was even more stubborn back then than I am now."

He chuckled. "No comment."

She turned back to him and smiled.

The first one he'd seen since they were reunited this morning, and it made his stomach flutter. He ignored it. *You can't give your heart to anyone. Remember your possible condition.*

"So, how did you find out about Leah?" He needed to stay on topic.

"I started contacting all adoption offices to find my biological parents but didn't have any success. My records were sealed for some strange reason, so I gave up. Until six months ago. I had an accident and needed a certain blood antigen. The doctors put a call out for it and a donor stepped forward."

"Leah."

Madi twirled her braid. "Well, I didn't know at first as they don't give out the information, but Brenda convinced me to take up my pursuit to discover more about the donor. She suggested it might lead me to my family. It was a long shot, but I thought it would be a good place to start."

"Brenda is still your live-in housekeeper in Saint Andrews?"

"Yes. She's family. Anyway, I contacted the media to tell them my story, and that I was looking for the person who saved my life. That I wanted to repay their kindness. They ran with the article and three days later, Leah contacted me. The rest is history."

Tucker turned right onto the road that would take them to Dolumhart. "Wow. That's amazing. It's true what they say."

"What's that?"

"That God works in mysterious ways."

She harrumphed. "I doubt it."

"What? I thought you—"

Crunch!

His unmarked vehicle lurched forward from the impact of a rear-end collision. He checked his rear-view mirror. A black pickup truck was on their tail. He stepped on the gas, but it was too late. The truck rammed them harder, thrusting his car across the grass median toward oncoming traffic.

Tucker held his breath and waited for impact.

Someone had followed them from the station and were now in pursuit.

How had they found them?

"Watch out!" Madison yelled and clutched the armrest until her fingers turned white.

"Grab my radio and call for backup!" Tucker swerved back across the median into their lane of the divided highway. He flipped on his lights and siren.

Madison pressed the button on Tucker's radio.

"CBSA officer Madison Steele requesting backup just off Route 1. Constable Tucker Reed and I took a hit from a black truck. They're still after us. Send all available units." She relayed the road marker.

"Officer Steele, police are en route to you," the dispatcher said.

Madison clicked off and tightened her grip on the armrest. She caught a glimpse of the truck in the side mirror. It approached again at full force, intent on slamming into the back of their vehicle. Where had the vehicle come from? Were they so wrapped up in their conversation, they hadn't spotted it? She chastised herself for not concentrating on solving her sister's murder and stopping the shipments of Morvecet across the New Brunswick–Maine border. "They're coming back."

"Hold on!" Tucker sped up and maneuvered into the right lane, dodging around another car.

The truck copied his moves and accelerated into the left lane beside them. Their window opened and a rifle appeared.

"Gun!" Madison yelled. Her erratic pulse matched the pounding in her head as fear took over. *Stay in control.*

Tucker hit the brakes and the cruiser's tires screeched. The vehicle swerved as he fought to maintain control.

Madison pointed to an upcoming exit. "Take that road! We need to get off the busy highway and not endanger lives."

Tucker sped up and at the last minute he steered onto the ramp, catching the assailants off guard. The pickup missed the exit and raced down the road. Tucker radioed his fellow officers, giving them the vehicle's description and where the truck was last seen.

Madison exhaled. "Close call. What do you think they wanted?"

"You."

"What? Why?"

"You became a target as soon as you found that flash drive. I'm guessing the people in the truck were the same ones who fired on us earlier. They're watching us."

A tingle darted over her arms, chilling her body. She closed her window. "Do you think they caused Leah's accident too?"

"Probably." The radio crackled with an update that officers spotted the truck and were in pursuit. "Good, maybe we'll get some answers once they catch them."

But would they? Madison's instincts told her these people—whoever they were—wouldn't be easy to apprehend. "Let's get to Dolumhart. I need answers."

Within minutes, they entered the five-story building housing the pharmaceutical company's satellite office and other local businesses. They stopped at the security desk.

"We're here to see Vice President Daniel Levine

of Dolumhart Pharmaceuticals." Tucker flashed his badge. "We don't have an appointment, but I believe he'll see us."

The young blond guard picked up his phone and placed a call, relaying the message. Seconds later, he returned the receiver to its cradle. "The receptionist said to come to the fifth floor. Elevator is around the corner to your right."

"Thank you," Madison said.

The elevator chimed as they arrived at the fifth floor. The duo walked through the double glass doors and entered the luxurious office adorned with mahogany furniture. They approached the front desk.

The attractive twentysomething receptionist flashed a flirty grin at Tucker. "Wow. I didn't realize St. Stephen had such handsome police officers. You must be new in town."

Madison flinched as a wave of jealousy skirted through her. Why? It was not like Tucker would ever forgive her for breaking his heart. Plus, after losing her fiancé to a heart attack on their wedding day eighteen months ago, Madison vowed to remain single forever. She barely survived Lucas Gagnon's death. She moved back to her Saint Andrews home from Quebec after requesting a transfer to the New Brunswick–Maine border. If it wasn't for Brenda Sorenson's constant watch care, Madison didn't know if she would have pulled through the pain. Her live-in housekeeper was more than an employee. She had practically raised Madison, especially after her parents' plane crash.

Tucker remained silent. The receptionist's comment caught him off guard.

Madison stepped forward and pulled out her identification. "I'm border patrol officer Madison Steele. This is police constable Tucker Reed. We're here to see Mr. Levine."

The woman leaned forward. "Wait. Aren't you Miss Peters's sister?"

"How did you know?"

"She talks about you all the time." The receptionist narrowed her eyes. "Very annoying. Anyway, where is she? She raced out of here earlier and hasn't returned."

They hadn't heard yet. Madison glanced at Tucker.

He picked up the woman's nameplate. "Annabelle, is it?"

"Yes, but you can call me Bella, handsome." She fluttered her fake eyelashes.

The woman was unbearable.

Tucker slammed her nameplate back on the desk. "Leah Peters died in a car accident a few hours ago."

"What? I'm so sorry."

"Thank you," Madison said. "You say she rushed out. Did she give you any indication why?"

Annabelle's glance turned toward Mr. Levine's

office and then downward. "No. She didn't even speak to me."

Her body language conveyed evasion. What was she hiding?

"We need to talk to Mr. Levine," Tucker said. "Now."

Annabelle picked up the phone and spoke to her boss before hanging up. "You can go in."

Tucker knocked and opened the door.

The silver-haired vice president stood. "Officers, what can I help you with?" His Italian-tailored dark suit personified extravagance along with his gold Rolex wristwatch.

Madison knew it well from seeing her CEO father in an Armani every day. Mr. Levine hadn't spared any cost in his attire. Would a vice president of a satellite office make that much money?

Tucker stepped forward. "Mr. Levine. I'm Constable Tucker Reed and this is CBSA border patrol officer Madison Steele."

His lips curled. "Leah's sister."

This man knew about her too? And why the animosity? "Yes."

Mr. Levine pointed to the plush leather chairs. "Have a seat."

Tucker pulled out his cell phone. "That won't be necessary." He scrolled and then held the screen in the man's direction. "Why would Miss Peters send this email to the CEO of Dolumhart and cc you?"

The man's eyes bulged. "I have no record of this email."

"And why did you doctor the clinical trial results of Morvecet?" Madison asked.

Tucker swiped his screen again and held it out. "Here's a copy of the tainted ingredients."

The older gentleman raised his hands into a stop position. "Again, I have no record of this."

"Show him a copy of the alarming test results." Madison was tired of this man's attitude.

Tucker once again scrolled and held out his iPhone. "Let me guess. You have no record of this either?"

"Nope. Our system crashed an hour ago. Wiped out many of our documents."

"How convenient," Madison said. "And I'm guessing it's all of the Morvecet files."

"Unfortunately, yes. However, I can assure you we used the best combinations of ingredients. I don't know what you're talking about and I told Miss Peters the same."

Madison stepped closer, getting into his personal space. "Did you order a hit on my sister? Did you kill her?"

The man stumbled backward, falling into his chair. "She's dead?"

"Yes, and I'm going to find out if you were involved." Madison waggled her finger at him.

He bolted upright and pointed at the door. "Get out! Both of you before I call Security."

"How dare you—"

Tucker took Madison's arm, nudging her toward the door and interrupting her statement. "Let's go," he said. He turned back to Mr. Levine. "We'll be back."

They made their way to the elevator, ignoring Annabelle on their exit.

Tucker punched the down button. "Madison, that was not professional."

She murmured and stepped into the elevator. "I know. I'm sorry. He just made me so angry."

"Please don't prove my boss right. Remember, I vouched for you. You need to remain strong." He hit the button to take them to the lobby.

She pulled her shoulders back. "I will prove they're lying. They're covering—"

The elevator plunged.

The force of the dive slammed Madison to the floor, her stomach dropping with it. Tucker's earlier words surfaced.

They're watching.

Madison's cell phone dinged, announcing a new text.

CONSIDER THIS A WARNING. STOP URE INVESTIGATION OR U'LL END UP LIKE URE SIS.

Madison fought for a breath, her anxiety threatening to expose her fear of the unknown. Her sister's death, the shooting, elevator plunge and now this text took its toll on her frame of mind.

Her sister's killer now wanted Madison and Tucker out of the way.

That meant they were getting closer to the truth, but would they survive this deadly drop?

FOUR

Fear stabbed Madison as panic zipped through her heart and lodged the scream she wanted to expel in her throat. The text only added to her terror-stricken state. Her mind raced back to the first time she'd gotten on a roller coaster and the horror that had overtaken her as it plummeted 245 feet to the ground. While all her friends loved it, she promised to herself she'd never go on another one again and hadn't. Until now, on this makeshift theme-park elevator ride. The numbers above the door descended rapidly and she braced for impact. Would this be how her life ended? On an elevator with her estranged childhood sweetheart? How ironic.

The emergency brakes kicked in and screeched their plunge to a suspended stop somewhere in between the first and second floors. The elevator bounced before stilling. Madison's labored breath threatened to worsen her panicked state, so she closed her eyes and inhaled deeply to calm herself. *You're okay.* It was not her time to die.

Only seconds had passed since they stepped into the elevator, but it seemed like they were frozen in time as they dropped.

"You okay?" Tucker had managed to stay upright, braced in the corner. He kneeled beside her and rubbed her arm.

Hadn't the drop scared him too? She couldn't

let him see her in a weakened state. She brushed away his touch and stood, rubbing her wobbly legs to bring life back into them. "I'm fine. We need to pry these doors open."

Tucker moved in front of her and pushed the right side of the door slightly to wedge his fingers between the cracks and shoved, grunting.

She couldn't help but admire his bulging muscles through his long-sleeved shirt. He'd worked out and buffed himself up in the last ten years.

He turned his head slightly. "Little help, please."

Right. *Quit staring.* She moved beside him, ignoring what his presence did to her, and pushed with all her strength.

Moments later they opened the doors only to find the elevator had stopped just a few feet shy of the current floor.

"I'll hold," Tucker said. "You climb up."

A scene from *Speed* flashed through her memory as a thought tumbled out. Would the brakes hold long enough? She wouldn't risk it and hastened her movements. She took a few steps back and rushed toward the opening, then jumped up onto the second floor. She thrust her arms forward and scrambled higher, using her feet against the elevator shaft.

The elevator-drop noise had attracted employees from the second floor, and someone helped her stand. "You okay?" a handsome blond man asked.

"Yes." She gestured to the small crowd. "Keep these doors open so Constable Reed can climb out."

Tucker hoisted himself upward but slipped.

She turned to the blond. "Can you help him?"

The man rushed forward and grabbed Tucker under the arm. "I've got you."

Madison held on to Tucker's opposite arm and they both pulled the constable from the suspended elevator.

They thanked the man and he returned to the gathering crowd.

Madison showed Tucker the text she'd received.

He pulled out his cell phone. "I'm calling it in. We need to get forensics over here." He moved closer to the group. "Everyone, this is now a crime scene. Please return to your offices."

The employees mumbled to each other before scrambling back into their places of employment.

Tucker spoke into his phone, requesting his leader send the forensics team to their location. "What? When?" The muscle cords in Tucker's neck protruded.

Something happened.

"Okay, we'll head over there. You send forensics here." Tucker paused. "I'm on it." His chilled voice conveyed irritation.

But why?

He clicked off the call and shoved his phone into his pocket. "Officers lost pursuit of the truck that rammed us." He paused and scratched the back of his neck. "Also, Hyatt is sending the forensics team here. We need to head to Allusions Hair Creations."

A knot formed in Madison's stomach. The salon's owner, Susan Stephens, had been cutting Madison's hair since she was a teenager and they'd formed a powerful bond throughout the years. Had something happened to the fun hairstylist?

Madison grabbed Tucker's arm. "Is Susan okay?"

"Don't know. A woman collapsed in the salon."

"So, why call you in? You're MCU."

"Not just me. You too."

Madison's jaw dropped. "Is it related to the case?"

"Appears that way. The woman who fainted is on Morvecet. Charlotte was the paramedic on-site and called Hyatt."

Great, not her nemesis again. Twice in one day was too much for Madison to deal with the irritating high school classmate. Charlotte had always tried to undermine Madison in front of Tucker. The woman's crush on him was clear. Then and now.

Why did Charlotte's earlier flirting bother Madison so much? It was not like there was still anything between Madison and Tucker. He'd never forgive her for what she did years ago, and she wouldn't open her heart again. Not after Lucas.

Madison swept off thoughts of past love and removed her cell phone. "I need to give my superintendent an update. When can we leave?"

"As soon as Forensics arrives."

Ten minutes later, they scrambled into Allusions Hair Creations and were greeted by the owner.

Madison rushed into the woman's arms. "Susan, I'm so glad you're okay. I was scared you were hurt."

The wavy-haired dirty-blonde pulled back from their embrace. "Sweet pea, I'm fine."

The woman's term of endearment always cheered Madison up. Even on the dark days.

Susan adjusted the waistline of her flowery paperbag pants before pointing to the woman on the floor. "Dolly here, not so much."

The paramedics hovered over Dolly, taking her vitals.

Tucker stepped forward. "Susan, good to see you again. Can you tell us what happened?"

"Well, hello love. I heard you were back in town. Your mama is tickled pink to have you home."

The cliché about hair salons was true, and Allusions was no exception. Especially in a small town. Over the years it became the area's source of information. Clients revealed their darkest secrets to Susan and she had the scoop before the residents of St. Stephen did.

"Dolly was complaining of a severe headache and when she got out from under the hair dryer, she collapsed. I called 911 and then Charlotte and Teddy arrived. They've been working on her ever since."

"Did she tell you what medication she was on?" Madison asked.

"That new one called Morvecet."

Tucker pulled out a notebook. "How long was she on it? Any other meds?"

"Just the past few weeks. She'd fallen down the stairs and wrenched her back. No other painkillers were helping. She'd heard of this new one and wanted to try it."

Tucker winced.

Madison knew what he was thinking. His mom.

A question logged in Madison's mind. How did Dolly get the drug since it wasn't on the shelves yet? Clearly, someone was distributing it.

Madison dug her nails into her palms to quench the growing anger from surfacing. Her sister died over the drug and now citizens were paying the price.

They had to stop Dolumhart.

And fast.

Tucker suppressed the uneasiness amplifying throughout his body. He needed to find out how his mother was doing. *Lord, please heal Mom. I can't lose her.* She was his rock. They'd been through many storms together.

Susan's cell phone buzzed and she glanced at the screen. "I gotta take this. Be right back." She stepped into her office.

"Tucker, over here please," Charlotte said.

He turned and caught her grin as he moved to where the seventysomething Dolly lay unconscious. Why did this paramedic's attitude feel like a pebble in his shoe—nonstop irritation?

You need to relax, Tucker. Concentrate.

He kneeled beside the paramedics. "Is she going to be okay? What happened?"

The heavy-set older man placed a drug bottle back into his bag. "Not sure yet. She came conscious for a minute and complained of major head pain, so I gave her morphine."

"Why that drug?" Tucker made a note.

"I don't have to justify my actions to you." He stood. "I'll get the gurney." He left without another word.

Charlotte grabbed Tucker's hand. "Don't mind Teddy. He's cranky today. Wife left him for a younger man. Now he's picking fights with everyone. Even me."

Madi came over to the group and cleared her throat. "Charlotte. Twice in one day. That's gotta be a record." She fisted her hands on her hips.

Tucker pulled away and stood. The irritation on Madi's contorted face niggled at him. Hadn't the two women been friends in high school? He knew they competed with each other but didn't remember the animosity between them.

Susan returned and hooked her arm through Madi's. "Is Dolly going to be okay, Charlotte?"

Charlotte's eyes clouded. "I don't know, Miss Susan."

"Charlotte, what made you contact Hyatt?" Tucker asked.

"Susan here told me Dolly confessed to being on Morvecet. That drug isn't available yet, so I thought I should report it quickly."

"Smart thinking. Did Dolly say anything to you before she went unconscious again?"

"Yes, but it was mumbled."

Susan sat cross-legged beside her patron, rubbing the older woman's arm. "She said, *Stop them.* What do you think that means?"

Tucker eyed Madi.

Her eyes widened before glancing his way.

He could almost hear her thoughts. This had to be related to her sister's death, especially if it was about Morvecet.

Susan sobbed quietly.

Madi pulled her into an embrace. "We'll find out, my friend."

"Thanks, sweet pea. Dolly is not only a customer of mine but a good friend. We walk together almost every night." Her voice quivered.

Teddy rushed through the door with the gurney in tow. "Move away, folks. We need to get her to the hospital."

Moments later, Charlotte and Teddy wheeled the patient toward the entrance.

Charlotte turned. "Handsome, if you want to

question her, you best get to the hospital quickly." She glanced at Susan. "Just in case."

The ambulance left with sirens blaring.

"Susan, is there anything else you can tell us? Did she say where she got the Morvecet?" Tucker made a note to ask his mother the same thing. If it wasn't available, where did she get it?

Susan twisted her lips. "Not sure." She fiddled with the belt on her flowy pants while biting her bright red lips.

What wasn't she telling them?

Madi touched the woman's arm. "Susan, you can tell us anything."

It impressed Tucker that her CBSA training taught her to read body language, so she also knew the salon owner held something back.

Susan huffed and walked back to her counter. "I don't know anything. If you will excuse me, I need to get back to work."

Tucker stepped forward. "But, you—"

Madi grabbed his arm. "It's okay, Susan. We'll leave you to it. I'll check on you later."

Tucker took the hint and fished a business card from his pocket, placing it on her desk. "Call if you remember any minor detail. Okay?"

The woman put in her earbuds and grabbed a mop without acknowledging his action.

Strange. He never remembered the eccentric hair stylist to be rude. Quirky, yes, but not rude. What had happened in the past ten years that he missed?

He followed Madi's quickened pace out of the salon. "What was that all about?"

She stopped at his vehicle and turned. "You don't have to pressure her. She just had a horrific experience."

He unlocked the cruiser. "She's holding something back."

"Please cut her some slack. She's been through a lot." Madi jumped in the passenger side.

He climbed in and started the engine. "What am I missing here?"

"Dolly is her best friend and Susan has helped her from tough spots."

"Like what?"

"Divorce. Drug addiction. Gambling."

Tucker pulled onto the road and headed toward Charlotte County Hospital. "Wow. No wonder Susan was protective. How do you know all this? Weren't you living in Quebec?"

"Yes, but Brenda kept me informed."

"So you never sold your house after you left? Why?"

Madi hit the button to roll the window down. The cool breeze ruffled her hair. "Couldn't part with it as I figured I'd be back one day."

"Can I ask you a question?"

"Sure."

"Why do you work? Your family must have left you well-off financially." Was he being too personal too soon?

"I love what I do. Protecting our borders is important to me." She flattened her lips. "Well, I also had to squash the rumors I was lazy and only wanted to live off my parents' money." She gazed out the window, ending their conversation.

He could take a hint. He had treaded into unwanted territory. Why did he care so much?

Moments later, they walked into the small-town hospital's entrance. "Let's hope Dolly is conscious now."

He stopped at the information center and flashed his badge. "We need to see Dolly..." He turned to Madi. "What's her last name?"

"Winters. Dolly Winters. She was just brought in by ambulance."

The receptionist's long nails flew across the keyboard. "She's still in Emerg." She hit the button to open the doors and pointed. "Follow the blue arrows."

Tucker rushed down the hallway and stopped at the nurse's station. "Constable Tucker Reed to see Dolly Winters. This is Officer Madison Steele."

"You family?" The silver-haired nurse pushed her glasses farther up her nose.

"No, but this is a police matter. We need to talk to her."

"It's okay, Francy." Charlotte sauntered over to the counter. "You can let them in. I'll vouch for him."

Francy gestured toward a closed-curtained stall. "Bed two."

Lethal Cover-Up

"Follow me," Charlotte said.

Tucker removed his hat. "How's she doing?"

The paramedic's eyes clouded. "Not good, I'm afraid."

"Has she regained consciousness?" Madi stepped beside them.

"Yes. The doc said they're taking her soon for a CT scan, so you must be quick." She slid the curtain aside.

Teddy rushed around the corner. "Charlotte, I've replenished our supplies. We need to leave." He bounced in one spot, clearly wanting to escape their company. Why?

Tucker and Madi entered the enclosed room.

Charlotte stood back.

The beeping heart monitor invaded the space.

Madi rushed past him and picked up the older woman's hand. "Dolly, it's me. Madison. How are you feeling?"

The woman groaned and licked her lips.

Tucker moved beside her bed. "Dolly, I'm police constable Tucker Reed. Can you tell me where you got the Morvecet?"

Dolly's cloudy eyes widened, revealing a panicked state.

Her lips moved, but nothing came out.

Madi leaned closer. "Dolly, you can tell us."

She opened her mouth. "They'll. Kill. Me." Her whispered, stuttered words could barely be heard over the machines.

"Who, Dolly?" Madi asked.

The woman raised a frail finger but dropped it quickly. Her weakened state evident.

Charlotte rushed forward and wrapped her hands around Dolly's. "You rest, love. The doctors will take good care of you."

Dolly closed her eyes, her lips turning blue.

The heart monitor screeched a flatlining beep.

Had they lost their lead to the distribution of Morvecet?

FIVE

"Everyone out now," the emergency doctor said. "Give us space."

Tucker backed out of the room along with the rest of the group. The medical team worked on Dolly, but after numerous jolts from the defibrillator, the young doctor stepped out from behind the curtain.

"I'm sorry," he said. "There was nothing we could do. She's gone."

Tucker pounded his fist against his thigh. Another senseless death. First Leah and now Dolly. When would it end? They needed answers, but whatever Dolly knew about the drug sellers died with her. Who was she referring to when she said they'd kill her? Dolumhart Pharmaceuticals?

It had to be. But how would they prove it? They needed more evidence.

Madi grabbed his arm. "She was our only lead right now. Other than what Leah copied onto the drive."

He pulled out his cell phone. "Maybe not. My mom might have information on the sellers. She's at a function, but I'll text and tell her I'm coming over later." He typed a message. "I'm also going to ask Hyatt to put a constable outside Mom's home. Just in case."

"Good idea." Madison checked her watch. "It's 4:30 already. Can you do me a favor and take me back to the station to get my car? I want to go see Susan before she leaves her shop. I need to tell her about Dolly in person before anyone else does."

"Sure." His phone chimed, and he glanced at the screen. "Text from Emerson. He's holding a press conference at 6:00 to talk about Leah's accident."

"What's he gonna say? Your team hasn't ruled it a homicide yet, even though we both know it is."

They moved out of Emerg and down the corridor, leaving the heartbreaking scene behind.

"No idea," Tucker said. "He's a good guy, but when he gets something in his head, there's no stopping him. He's on a warpath now."

He stepped through the sliding doors into the cool predusk temperatures and breathed in the fall air. It was his favorite time of year.

"Well, maybe his conference will help our investigation," Madi said.

"Either that or hinder it." He pulled the key fob out of his pocket and hit the button. "Let's get you back to your car. We'll continue our sleuthing tomorrow at 7:30 a.m. Sound good?"

She nodded.

An hour later, Tucker dried the last plate and placed it in his mother's cupboard, pondering today's events.

"Earth to Tucker," his mother said.

He'd almost forgotten her presence in the small kitchen. She'd finished wiping the table and stepped beside him. "What's going on?"

He turned to see the concerned expression on her pretty face.

Even after years of being apart, Beverley Reed always sensed when her son was troubled. The petite silver-streaked brunette rubbed Tucker's shoulder.

"I'm sorry, Mom. Just thinking about this case and what Madi must be going through."

She swatted his arm. "What? You didn't tell me anything earlier about Madison. You're working with her?"

Great, now his mother would interrogate him. "Yes."

"How is she?"

"Fine, considering she just lost the sister she'd only recently met."

His mom smiled and plugged in the teakettle. "Still a spark between you two?"

"A tense one. Mom, I don't want any relationships, let alone one with the woman who stomped all over my heart." He'd taken the breakup badly and his mother had tried her hardest to pull him from the pit he'd fallen into. Could he really have been that in love as a teenager? Seeing Madison today brought all the feelings back like it only happened yesterday.

Her eyes darkened. "You need to get tested, son. Just because your father had Huntington's doesn't mean you do."

His mother still read her son like a book.

Tucker clenched his jaw. He couldn't deal with this right now. He had other concerns tormenting him. "Mom, you know how I feel."

She sighed and grabbed a teabag. "God's got this."

"He does, but I just can't go there." With the recent news of his father's death and discovering his condition, Tucker hadn't come to terms with it yet. Why wouldn't his father have stayed with them when he'd found out? What was that saying in marriage vows? In sickness and in health. Didn't that also apply to children?

"Mom, why did Dad leave us? We could have helped."

She paused midstream in opening the tea package, a twisted expression forming on her face. "I begged him to stay, but nothing I said would convince him otherwise. He told me he had to be by himself. That he didn't want us to watch him deteriorate." She went back to preparing her tea. "You men and your pride."

Tucker gripped the sides of the countertop, his knuckles turning white. He needed to change the subject and put his anger toward his father aside. "Question for you. Where did you get the drug Morvecet? And why take an unapproved drug?" Oops. He hadn't meant to allow his irritation to creep into his tone.

She chewed her upper lip. A nervous habit she'd had for years.

He stroked her arm. "You can trust me."

"But you're a cop."

And she was his mother. Could he hold back information because of his love for her?

"Mom, people are dying from this drug. If you know something that can help with this case, tell me. I promise I'll protect you as much as I can."

And he would. He couldn't lose her too.

She finished tearing the tea package and plunked the bag into her cup of boiling water. "Son, I needed relief from the pain. Nothing else worked. That's the only reason I agreed to it."

"To what?"

She turned. "The exchange."

"With whom?"

"Not sure. Dolly gave me the number to text. She said to tell them how much I wanted and then wait."

Tucker reached for her hand. "Wait for what?"

"A location to hand off the money. They instructed me to put it in a brown paper bag and leave it there. Then they'd text me the drop-off site."

What? It sounded like some sick spy movie. "So you don't know who is selling you the Morvecet?"

She shook her head as a tear escaped. "I'm sorry, son. The pain was just so bad and Dolly told me it worked."

Dolly? Had she been the seller?

He pulled her into his arms. "It's okay, Mom. We'll work it out."

An idea formed.

Could he risk it and set up a sting using his mother?

After picking up her sedan and stopping by to give Susan the bad news, Madison pulled into the driveway of her home on the Saint Croix River in Saint Andrews, New Brunswick. Even though she had a thirty-minute work commute every day, she didn't mind as the peacefulness of her oasis was worth the drive.

Susan had collapsed into her arms when Madison told her about Dolly's death. The woman lost a dear friend and would miss their daily walks. Susan had pleaded with Madison to find the culprits and bring them to justice. She also apologized for her abruptness earlier. She confessed to letting her anger over Dolly's condition get the best of her emotions.

Could Madison uncover the person responsible? This was the first time she'd been involved with an investigation of this magnitude. Sure, she'd helped local police departments bring down smugglers and had recently stopped a major heroin ring, but this case already had two deaths. On the first day.

How many more would be lost before they solved the puzzle?

She stepped out of her vehicle, waving to the neighbor across the cul-de-sac. Her lavish house sat at the end of the street on the Saint Croix River's edge. A small lighthouse rested close to her home and added a protective ambiance to the area. Madison loved to spend the early mornings on the small beach, listening to the waves crash against the shoreline. It was her haven.

Madison opened the stained-glass doors and stepped into the white marble foyer of her home. Her gray kitten jumped off the deacon's bench and circled through her legs. She picked the fluffy animal up and kissed its forehead. "Hey, Squeaky. You glad to see me?"

The furry girl meowed as if in response.

Madison scratched under her chin and was rewarded with loud purrs. The stray had come to the Steele home two weeks ago. Madison found the thin kitten asleep on the back patio and couldn't bear to leave the poor thing out in the cold. She always was a sucker for the underdog.

Madison released Squeaky and the kitten scurried under the foyer table. "I'm home, Bren."

Brenda Sorenson had lived with the Steele family since Madison was a young child. After Welland and Dawn Steele had died, Brenda stayed at Madison's request. Madison had not only learned about her adoption but had lost her parents—all in one week. No wonder she no longer trusted in God.

What kind of God would allow all that to happen at once to a young girl? Not one she wanted to follow.

"I'm in the kitchen," Brenda said.

Garlic and mixed spices permeated the air the closer Madison got to the large open-concept kitchen and family room area. She kissed Brenda's cheek and pulled out a bar stool from the island. The television aired the news in the background.

"What's for supper? Smells delish." Madison placed her elbows on the counter and cupped her chin into her hands.

"Chicken pasta with fennel bulb." Brenda winked. "Your fave."

Madison's stomach growled at the mention of the yummy dish.

They laughed.

"Seems like you made it home just in time." Brenda tossed her spoon in the sink and embraced Madison. "I'm so sorry about Leah."

Pent-up tears cascaded down Madison's cheeks. They flowed freely in the solace of her home. "I miss Sissy already. I feel like I barely got to know her."

"Thankfully, God gave you some time."

Madison bristled. "God? He's now taken everything from me." She stood and walked to the large window overlooking the river. A sailboat drifted by.

Brenda returned to the stove and stirred the pasta. "Love, it's time to come back to Him."

Madison bit the inside of her cheek. She wouldn't take her frustration out on the beloved housekeeper who was more like family. "I don't want—"

Her cell phone buzzed in her pocket. Tucker. "Hey, what's going on?"

"Hyatt called. You were right. Leah was murdered."

Madison rubbed the back of her neck. "How do you know?"

"Her SUV was new, but the brakes weren't. Someone replaced them with faulty ones."

She drew in a ragged breath. "What? How would they have done that?"

"You'd be surprised at how innovative criminals are."

The television flashed to a scene with a picture of Emerson Peters behind the news anchor.

Madison moved closer to the screen. "Do you think this is why Emerson is holding a press conference?"

"Not sure how he found out before me. Perhaps Hyatt told him."

"Maybe."

"We're going live now with party representative Emerson Peters in St. Stephen," the woman said on the television. "Bob Fuller is reporting from town hall. Bob?"

Madison gestured to Brenda, snapping her fingers. "Turn it up, please." She plunked herself into the comfy teal sofa, curling her legs up. "Gotta run, Tucker. Chat later."

"Before you go. A cruiser will be driving by

your home throughout the night. I'm not taking any risks. See you tomorrow." He ended the call.

Madison grimaced.

Brenda increased the volume. "Tucker? As in Tucker Reed?"

Madison shoved her phone onto the glass coffee table. "Yes, I'm working with him on this case."

She clucked her tongue. "You failed to state that information earlier. I didn't realize he was back in town."

"Don't start. Shhh and listen."

Brenda smirked and sat in the oversize rocker.

A short, plump man appeared on the screen with a crowd behind him. "Thanks, Carla. We're here live with Emerson Peters for an announcement. Let's listen to what he has to say."

The camera switched to a podium on the steps of town hall. Emerson, dressed in a dark navy suit, stood with an entourage beside him. He moved closer to the mic and cleared his throat. "Thank you for coming. I wanted to tell the people of my hometown some tragic news."

He paused and bit his lip.

Not a normal action for the composed and bold politician.

Well, at least as far as Madison knew. She'd only met him once, but Leah had told her ample about her father.

"My beloved daughter, Leah Peters, was murdered today."

A collective gasp sounded from the crowd. The statement Tucker posed a few minutes ago came back to her mind. How *had* Emerson heard about the tampered brakes? The question bothered her.

Then again, didn't most politicians have constituents in high places?

The shot focused in and Emerson's eyes narrowed. "I will not stop until I put the culprits behind bars." He waggled his finger at the camera. "Whoever you are, you will not get away with this. My good friend, Constable Tucker Reed, and my stepdaughter, Madison Steele, will catch you."

Madison jerked her legs back onto the floor and leaned forward.

"Mr. Peters, we didn't realize you had a stepdaughter. Who is she?" The reporter moved closer and thrust his mic into Emerson's face.

"Yes, she recently came into my life. She's a border patrol officer and is working with Tucker on a joint task force."

Did Tucker tell him that?

Madison fisted her fingers. She wasn't sure she liked him knowing her business.

"You mean you didn't know about Officer Steele?"

"No, I didn't. She's my deceased wife's daughter from a previous relationship. I'm looking forward to getting to know Madison."

Emerson's expression changed for a split second, but Madison caught it.

Was it anger that passed over his handsome face? If so, why?

Another reporter stepped forward. "Why do you think someone would kill your daughter? To stop you from running for leadership of your party?"

"Well, if they did, it won't work. Nothing will stop me. Mark my words. I *will* become premier of this province." His tone conveyed something.

Malice? Determination?

Emerson raised his hands. "That's all, folks." He stepped away from the podium and walked into the building.

A timer dinged.

Brenda turned the television off. "Supper's ready."

Two hours later, after a soothing bath and adding a long comfy sweater over her pajamas, Madison sipped a decaf pumpkin-spice latte in her cozy sunroom. One of her favorite places. The fire-orange sun disappeared over the horizon, bringing with it a spectacular glistening prism effect on the water. She picked up the latest James Rollins suspense thriller. A relaxing way to unwind after a hectic day. Well, as much as was possible with her favorite writer. His action-packed stories pulled her in every time.

The doorbell rang.

Moments later, Brenda rushed into the sunroom holding a box. "Parcel for you left at the door. The driver took off before I could thank them. Look who it's from." She placed it on the coffee table.

Madison turned the box to view the return address.

Leah Peters.

An envelope addressed with "Sissy" on it was taped to the top.

The room spun and Madison grabbed the sofa's armrest to steady herself.

Had Leah sent this in prediction of her own death?

"She must have made arrangements before noon when she called me." It was the only explanation. Wasn't it? Madison removed the envelope before grabbing a pair of scissors. She sliced through the packing tape, her heart thumping in apprehension of what she would find.

Brenda's eyes widened. "You don't think she anticipated her death, do you?"

Madison shrugged. "Nothing at this point would surprise me after such a horrific day." She opened the box and peeked inside.

She chuckled at what appeared.

A teddy bear lay on top with a note attached to his plaid bow tie. Madison picked it up and squeezed. "He's so cute and cuddly."

"But why would she send you a bear? You're not a stuffed-animal kind of woman."

"But she is...was." Madison choked back a sob and gulped in a big breath to stop her tears. She'd save them for later. "This one was her fave. His name is Winston. She said he was special."

Madison unfastened the safety pin and removed the envelope but set it aside. She would read it in the solitude of her bedroom later.

Brenda picked up the bear. "Why was it special to her?"

"Our mother gave it to her when she was a baby." Madison shifted her attention back to the box.

Tissue paper secured with jute hid the remaining contents. Was her sister sending her a gift or something more? Curious, she cut the rope and removed the paper.

And froze.

Her sister's gold laptop sat on top along with various papers and another sealed envelope with her full name written on it.

In a handwriting Madison didn't recognize.

She picked it up and traced the cursive script with her finger. Who was this from?

"Why would she send you a laptop? You have one."

Brenda's question interrupted her curiosity over the note and Madison set it back down. "That's her personal laptop."

"But why send it to you?"

Could there be more evidence on it she didn't want anyone else to see? More than what was on the flash drive?

"Good question, Bren. It's almost like she felt she was going to die." What would it be like to know that? Madison had always feared the unknown. She tried hard not to think about it too much as it put her in panic mode, but ever since she was a kid the thought of dying plagued her. Brenda had tried to instill in her to trust in God, but Madison had been hurt too much to allow someone unseen in her life.

Madison checked the wall's sailboat clock—8:30 p.m. Almost time for bed. She was an early-to-bed, early-to-rise kind of person. She packed everything back into the box. "It's been a long day. I think I'll take this to my room and crash."

Brenda kissed her cheek. "Understand. Night, love. Try to have a good sleep."

"You too."

After brushing her teeth, Madison walked across the warmed hardwood floor and sat on her bed. She pulled Winston from the box and hugged him, smiling at her sister's obsession of teddy bears. Madison fingered him before setting him on the nightstand.

Squeaky jumped up on her bed, circled Madison twice before cuddling on her pillow.

Madison chuckled and picked up Leah's note as a wave of nausea rose, threatening to overpower her with trepidation. She inhaled deeply and opened the envelope.

Dear Sissy,

If you're reading this letter, I've been murdered. I arranged with a close friend to deliver it upon my death. I'm so sorry for the anguish you're probably going through right now. Please know this, I'm with my heavenly Father and at peace.

Peace? Hardly. Madison clutched the paper more firmly and kept reading.

I'm leaving you a letter from Mama, work papers, my laptop and my special teddy bear. There's more incriminating evidence on the laptop and another coded message somewhere on it. Sorry for the secrecy, but I needed to do this in case it fell into the wrong hands. It's password protected with my teddy's name and the day and month of our first meeting.

You're the best thing that has happened to me in years. I praise God for you. Come back to Him…before it's too late.

Sissy, I love you to infinity and beyond,
Leah xo
#SistersForever

Madison's breath hitched before sobs overtook her body. Why had God taken everyone she loved away from her? She could never—

Boom!

An explosion shook her home, followed by a loud roar. She stiffened. What was that? Squeaky bolted off the bed, scampered under it to escape the noise. Madison grabbed her cell phone and raced to the bedroom window.

A fiery inferno engulfed her neighbor's home. She put on her housecoat and rushed through the house, calling 911 to request fire trucks to their cul-de-sac.

Brenda joined her and they ran out the front door.

Even the distance between their houses couldn't squash the heat from the fire.

Madison stepped forward, but Brenda jerked her back. "It's too late. The house is gone."

"But Doreen and Bert are in there." The thought of the sweet older couple perishing crushed Madison.

"No, they're not. They left after supper for a getaway. Thank God."

Air swooshed out of her lungs. *Yes, indeed.*

Her text chimed an alert and she checked the screen.

A picture of her and Brenda watching the fire appeared.

C HOW CLOSE WE CAN GET TO U. STOP INVESTIGATING. THIS IS YOUR FINAL WARNING.

She inhaled sharply and glanced around.

A crowd formed on their tiny street.

Could the suspect be among them?

A question popped into her head as sirens pierced the night.

What had she done getting involved with this task force?

No one was safe.

SIX

Tucker lay in bed, flipping the pages of his favorite jet magazine, not really seeing the words before him. He huffed and threw it aside. He couldn't concentrate as his mind raced back to Emerson's press conference. Something bothered him about it. Hyatt had told Tucker he didn't update the politician regarding his daughter's brakes.

So, if he hadn't, who had?

He grabbed his cell phone and texted Jenkins to find out if it was him.

A single-word reply came back.

Nope.

Then who did?

His phone buzzed. Madi. He sat upright. Why was she calling this late?

He hit Answer. "What's wrong, Madi?" He grimaced at the use of her nickname, but it rolled off his tongue too easily.

"They set my neighbor's house on fire." Her panicked voice elevated his guard.

His stomach tightened. "What? Who?"

"Not sure. I'm sending a screenshot of the text I got."

Seconds later his cell phone dinged, and he switched the screen to see what she'd sent.

A picture of her and Brenda watching the fire with a threatening caption.

He threw his comforter back and jumped out of bed. "On my way. Lock your doors and stay inside. Do you have your gun?"

"Yes, my superintendent gave me permission to bring it home since I'm on the task force. We're behind locked doors. The firemen are here, but I'm not sure how much is salvageable."

"I'll be there as fast as I can."

Twenty minutes later at record speed, Tucker drove around the fire trucks and pulled into Madi's lane.

The firemen had extinguished the flames, and a soot-infested frame was all that remained. Smoke still rose from the pile of carnage. Tucker sent up a quick prayer for the family. Had they been able to get out in time?

He turned back to Madi's home and rushed out of his vehicle. He'd check with the fire chief later on whether they've determined the cause. First, he had to ensure Madi and Brenda were okay.

Before he could ring the doorbell, the stained-glass doors opened and Madi stumbled into his arms.

"I'm so glad you're here," she said. "This is getting too real and now I'm putting Bren at risk. Where was the constable you said would be patrolling the area?" Her voice quivered.

Good question. He squeezed her tighter, liking

how it felt to once again have her in his arms. *Don't go there, Tucker. Remember how she crushed your heart.*

"Probably on a call." He broke away from their embrace. "It's gonna be okay. Let's go inside."

She nodded and stepped back into the house.

He followed and took in the surroundings. "Wow, you've done some redecorating since I've been here. It's beautiful."

"Thank you. I renovated when I moved back from Quebec eighteen months ago. I needed to take my mind off—"

She stopped.

Her mind off what? What happened in Quebec that brought her home again?

"Tucker!" Brenda raced around the corner and hugged him. "So good to see you."

He chuckled. "You too, Brenda. How've you been?"

"Getting old. Let me look at you." She backed up and held him at arm's length, clucking her tongue. "Could it be possible for you to be even more handsome?"

"You haven't lost your sense of humor, have you?" Tucker moved farther into the foyer.

"Never. How about a tea?"

"Sure but give me a few minutes to check the house and grounds. I want to be sure no one is lurking."

"Did she tell you about the box she received from Leah tonight?" Brenda asked.

"What? No." He turned to Madi. "What did she send you?"

Madi shifted her stance. "Later. Did you talk to the fire chief about the cause of the fire?"

"Not yet. Let me check and I'll also do a perimeter sweep. You ladies stay inside." He didn't wait for a reply and stepped into the night.

A heavy scent of charred wood assaulted his nose, and he coughed. The pungent smoke smell would linger in the air for a bit. Tucker approached the closest firefighter and flashed his badge. "Can I talk to the person in charge?"

The man pointed to another fireman walking through the wreckage. "That's Chief Forester."

"Thanks," Tucker said and moved in the man's direction.

The chief raised his hands in a stop position. "Whoa, stay back."

Tucker stopped and held out his badge. "Constable Tucker Reed of the Major Crimes Unit. I need to talk to you about this fire."

The man stepped over the debris and held out his hand. "Chief Bob Forester. MCU, huh? Why are you here?"

"I'm working with a joint task force with CBSA border patrol officer Madison Steele." He pointed to her house. "She lives across the street. I believe this fire was set to scare her into giving up our investigation into her sister's murder today."

Forester adjusted his helmet. "You mean, Leah Peters?"

"You heard?"

"I assumed you meant the politician's daughter. When he speaks, everyone listens." Sarcasm laced his words.

The man wasn't wrong. Emerson knew how to capture an audience, but the tone in Forester's voice insinuated something other than respect. Hatred? Disgust?

"You don't like Mr. Peters?"

He scowled. "Not particularly. Anyway, I can tell you this. The fire here? Was deliberately set."

Not surprised. "Was there anyone inside?"

"No, neighbors reported that the older couple already left on vacation."

Thank the good Lord. "Can you tell me how you concluded it wasn't an accident so soon into your investigation?"

"See that truck in the wreckage?" He pointed to the charred classic pickup sitting halfway into the burnt house.

"Is that a '69?"

"Good eye. This truck struck a gas line and caused the explosion."

"The driver?" Tucker asked.

"Was none."

"What?" Tucker edged closer. There wasn't much

left, including a license plate. Dead end. "How do you know it was used to ram the house?"

Forester bent over and picked up three items. A brick, steel bar and a singed bungee cord. "Found these inside it. Someone rigged the gas pedal."

"Knowing they'd probably hit the gas line."

"Easy to do. I'm sure the fire marshal will agree with me that this was arson. Sure and simple."

"Thank you for your time." Tucker pulled out a business card. "Can you have him call me to confirm it for sure and advise if you find anything else in the ruins?"

"Absolutely."

Tucker stuffed his notebook back into his pocket and pulled out a Maglite. He wanted to check the surrounding area for evidence of the suspect watching Madi's house. Plus, he needed to ensure her property was secure.

He walked around the house, checking windows and shining the light to look for any disturbances or footprints. Nothing.

The suspect was probably long gone by now.

Tucker made his way to the property's edge and the gate that led down to the beach. It, too, was secure.

His flashlight beam caught the lighthouse's outline to the right of Madi's home. He walked over to it and circled it, inspecting as he went.

At the back of the small lighthouse, he stopped as something drew his eye.

Cigarette butts.

Lots of them.

A tremor snaked up his back. How long had the suspect been watching Madi's house?

One thing was evident.

She'd been targeted.

Madison followed Tucker's movements to the lighthouse from the sunroom's window wall. He lingered at the back. Had he found something? She rubbed her eyebrow as her chest tightened and the words from the text replayed in her mind like an old scratched LP record stuck in unending repetition. *This is your final warning.* Had they watched her from the lighthouse—a place supposedly personifying shelter?

Tucker reappeared with a bag in his hand and walked around, then entered the front door. "I'm back."

She rushed to meet him. "What did you find?"

He held up the bag. "Cigarette butts."

"But they could be from any one of my neighbors. Plus, we often get people walking down the cul-de-sac to the lighthouse."

"This many though? They were all in one spot with a perfect view of your house."

Madison swayed and grabbed the door frame to steady herself.

Tucker set the bag on the foyer table and squeezed her shoulder. "I don't like it either. This hits too close to home. Your home. I'll make sure the constable is stationed outside from now on instead of patrolling the area. I need you safe."

His simple gesture sent familiar goose bumps skimming over her arms. Had her teenage crush returned so quickly? Or perhaps it never left.

She couldn't succumb to old feelings. She pulled her shoulders back and stepped away. "I'll be fine. I have a great security system."

Something flashed in his eyes. Disappointment from her withdrawal?

Or something else?

She pushed the question from her mind and moved into the kitchen where Brenda set cups on the island.

Tucker followed. "Do you have video surveillance?"

"No need out here."

He crossed his arms. "I beg to differ. After everything that's happened today, it's evident they've targeted you."

Brenda fumbled with the sugar bowl. "What do you mean?"

"The fire chief told me that someone rigged a truck to plow into your neighbor's house. It hit a gas line and caused the explosion. Plus, from your text it's clear they're watching you."

"Love, do you think they found out Leah sent you something they want?" Brenda filled the kettle with water.

"What did she send you?" Tucker asked.

Madison sat on an island bar stool. "Her personal laptop and documents."

"Okay, we need to take it into evidence," Tucker said.

"No!" Madison flinched. She didn't mean to yell, but she hadn't checked to determine if there was anything personal on it for her eyes only. "We don't know the contents and I'm not sure I trust anyone but us."

"Okay, how about we look at it here? Now."

Brenda dumped the water from the teakettle and grabbed the carafe. "I think you're gonna need leaded coffee instead."

After retrieving Leah's laptop, Madison and Tucker sat at the dining room table sipping coffee. She opened the mac.

A password box appeared.

"Great. Now what?" Tucker asked.

"She gave me a hint that only I would know. Her teddy bear's name and the day and month we first met."

"Which is?"

Madison typed in *Winston0323*.

The laptop beeped with an access denied message.

"What? Winston is the bear's name and we met on March twenty-third." The annoying sound made her want to throw the computer across the room. Why couldn't anything go right today?

"Did you type in letters or numbers for the date?"

Madison face-palmed her forehead. "Right. Let me try something else."

She entered *WinstonMarch23*.

The computer sprung to life.

Madison held her hand in the air. "Yes."

They high-fived.

A smirk tugged at the corners of Tucker's mouth.

"What's so funny?"

He drank from his mug. "Nothing. Just realized how much I've missed our friendship."

Me too. However, she wouldn't admit that. Not to him or herself. She had to stay focused. Plus, if she got too close, she couldn't guarantee where her feelings would end up. Something had sparked between them earlier, but the hurt over Lucas's death was too painful for her to let her guard down. She had spent many nights crying herself to sleep. Her heart had barely recovered from the loss. After Tucker found out what she'd done, it would only end in torture and she refused to go through that again.

"Okay, let's see what's on here." She shifted the screen so Tucker could also peruse the file folders. "Looks like mostly personal information."

Tucker pointed to a file marked DP. "Does that stand for Dolumhart Pharmaceuticals?"

"Not a very clever disguise." She clicked on it and several files popped on the screen. She scrolled through them. "Yup, these are the same as what she put on the flash drive. Nothing new."

Tucker finished his coffee and took the mug to the sink. "I don't understand why she would be so secretive and send you her laptop if it's the same information. What are we missing?"

Madison cupped her hands behind her head and leaned back. Her weary body needed sleep soon, or she'd never be able to get up in the morning. "Time to call it a night? Perhaps fresh eyes would—"

A folder caught her eye and she popped forward. "No way."

Tucker rushed back to the table. "What?"

She pointed to the folder. "Look at the label."

"2I&B? What does that mean?"

"We used to sign our emails with that. It means to infinity and beyond as in I love you to the moon and back." Her sister was leading her to this file. Madison's knee bounced. This had to be their break in the case.

"This file was disguised so only you would know the meaning?"

"Yes. Let's check it out." She doubled clicked on the folder. One Word document appeared. A personal message? Should she look at it in front of Tucker? She hovered over the mouse, but after seconds of contemplation, opened it. A single sentence appeared.

Sissy, you will find more incriminating evidence in a place where I find comfort.

Madison slouched in her chair. "My sister always

liked a good treasure hunt, but this is absurd." She rubbed her eyes. "I have no idea what this means."

Tucker tapped his fingers on the table. "Where did she live?"

"A townhouse in St. Stephen and I know where she hid the key."

"Maybe she hid it there in a favorite spot?"

"That has to be it." Madison closed the laptop. "A puzzle for tomorrow. I need sleep."

Tucker stood. "I'll be calling for patrol cars to check your house."

"Is that necessary?" Madison took her mug to the sink.

"Yup." He headed to the foyer. "Please lock up after me and set your alarm."

She saluted him and giggled. "Yes, sir!" When was the last time she'd giggled like a schoolgirl? Ages ago. Sure, Leah and she had moments when they'd laugh so hard, they cried, but lately her sister had seemed so uptight. Why hadn't Madison noticed and asked?

Maybe Leah would be alive today if she had.

Tears threatened, but she bit them back. There would be plenty of time to cry later. Right now she had to solve the case and catch her sister's killer.

"Shall we meet at the Border Junction Café at 7:30?" Tucker asked.

"Sounds good." She opened the door for him. "Bye."

After brushing her teeth, Madison crawled into

bed beside a sleeping Squeaky and eyed the box from Leah. It would have to wait till tomorrow. Her exhausted brain couldn't take any more today.

She grabbed Winston from the stand and hugged him, a waft of lilac permeating her nose. Leah's scent. She breathed in as a tear escaped. *Sissy, I miss you already. Why did you have to leave me all alone?*

You're not alone. I'm here.

What? Where had that thought come from?

A fall wind howled outside her bedroom window, bringing with it a storm brewing inside her. She crawled farther under the covers and hugged Winston as if he'd protect her from the monsoon of wickedness thrust into her small-town life.

Where would she find safety?

SEVEN

Madison shuffled into the Border Junction Café fifteen minutes before her scheduled time to meet Tucker. Her sluggish body ached from a restless sleep and yesterday's taxing day, and she needed a special treat to give her a boost. The aroma of roasting coffee beans tickled her senses and perked her adrenaline. She glanced around the small vintage café nestled between Allusions Hair Creations and an antique shop on St. Stephen's main downtown street. Patrons already filled most tables. It was a popular spot to chat, work, read or interview for jobs.

"Well, fancy meeting you here this early."

Madison tensed at the familiar female's raspy voice.

Charlotte.

She rustled up a cheerful expression and turned. "Morning. Time for your daily coffee fix?"

The paramedic pulled a folded ten-dollar bill from her pocket. "Yup. Gonna be another busy one. Where's your handsome sidekick?"

Madison bristled. Why did competitive memories rush her whenever Charlotte was around? She needed to let it go. Elsa popped into her head. Great, now she'd have that song mulling around all day.

The door's bells jingled, announcing another patron.

Tucker.

Madison's pulse hitched at the sight of her gorgeous friend.

Friend? They were once much more and had talked about marriage—even as teenagers. She set aside the conversation they'd had in his old tree house many years ago and focused on today. Getting to the bottom of her sister's death was top priority, not old love.

Charlotte squealed. "We were just talking about you. Handsome, let me buy *you* a coffee."

Did she actually emphasize the word *you* and squeal all in one breath? Were they back in high school?

Madison caught Tucker's pinched expression cross over his face seconds before his lips curved upward into an obvious forced smile.

The thought of his annoyance toward Charlotte brought joy. Wow. Did she just think that? She had—

Her cell phone played the theme to *Jaws.* Her superintendent's favorite movie. She stepped away and hit Answer. "Morning, boss." His random call only meant one thing.

Something happened.

She braced for bad news.

"You and Constable Reed need to get over to the Ferry Point Crossing. A trucker tried to go around barriers to cross the bridge when border patrol told him to turn around. Agents detained him back at the Calais station in Maine."

This border crossing was only for automobiles, so why had the trucker not known that?

"But why us?"

"He was driving a Dolumhart Pharmaceuticals truck and said he wants to talk to Madison Steele."

Madison rubbed her temple, trying to ward off a tension headache already. "How does he know me?"

"The press conference, remember? Peters said your name."

Right.

"We'll be there shortly."

"You better wrap up this case soon. I need you back on your booth." He clicked off.

No pressure.

She suppressed a sigh at her leader's attitude and turned to Tucker, waving her phone. "That was my boss. We need to grab our coffees and roll."

He nodded and stepped up to the counter.

Ten minutes later after dropping her sedan off at Tucker's station, they crossed the bridge into Calais, Maine, and pulled into the U.S. Customs and Border Protection station.

A six-foot male U.S. border patrol agent stood outside the entrance. He waved them in.

Madison stepped from the car and held out her hand. "Wyatt, good to see you again."

Wyatt returned the gesture. "How are you, Madison?"

"Great." She pointed to Tucker. "This is police constable Tucker Reed. We're working on a joint task force to catch this drug ring."

Wyatt nodded. "Nice to meet you. Superintendent Watson said you were coming together. We have the trucker inside." He held the door open.

Madison entered. "I heard you were moving."

"Back to my family's ranch in Montana. Heading home tomorrow." He led them down a corridor.

"That's quick," Madison said. "Sorry to see you go."

"My sister passed and I need to take care of my niece. She has no one."

Madison grabbed his arm. She could relate to his loss with all the death she'd gone through. "I'm so sorry."

"Thanks." He held the doorknob. "Your driver is in here. Name's Brian Brown from Minto, New Brunswick." He held a file out to Tucker. "His information is in here."

"Any priors?" Tucker asked as he opened the folder.

"We couldn't find anything on him. So, unless he's using an alias, he's clean."

Tucker glanced at the file and handed it to Madison. "Did he say why he was trying to cross at the wrong border?"

"He's been tight-lipped. He'll only speak with Madison."

Why her? Sure, Emerson mentioned her name, but it wasn't like she had any leeway in helping him. "Let's meet him and see what we can find out."

Wyatt opened the door. "He's all yours."

A bushy-bearded redhead slouched behind the table, chewing his gum. "'Bout time you got here."

Madison flexed her hands and sat. She already didn't like the guy's attitude. "I'm CBSA officer Madison—"

"I know who you are." He scowled. "You're my ticket out of here."

Tucker turned around a chair and straddled it in front of Brian. "Stop interrupting the lady and tell us why you tried to evade instructions and cross this border."

Brian tugged at his beard. "I ain't talkin' to you, Constable Reed."

He knows Tucker too? Was this man connected to the distribution of Morvecet?

"Okay, tell me why you tried to cross the barrier," Madison said.

"I want a deal and only you can get it for me."

She opened the file. "Is Brian Brown your real name? I find it hard to believe you have no record."

His eyes darkened. "Give me a deal and I'll tell you."

"How can I give you a deal?"

"You're connected with the supposed next premier of New Brunswick. Surely, Emerson Peters can get me off."

Wyatt rested against the wall. "What have you done that you need help? It's obvious running around a barricade is not the only misdemeanor you've committed."

Brian slammed his hand on the table and stood. "I ain't talking to you." He shoved his finger in Tucker's face. "Or you!"

Tucker bolted out of his chair. "That's it. I'm placing you under arrest." He turned Brian around and cuffed his hands behind his back before shoving him into the chair.

The man cursed. "On what charge?"

Tucker sat. "How about assaulting a police officer?"

Madison suppressed a chuckle. Even after ten years apart, she could still tell when Tucker was bluffing. The slight twitch in his lower lip was always his undoing when he wasn't being totally honest.

Brian's eyes bulged. "That's a lie! I ain't ever assaulted no one."

"Well then, cooperate. Why do you want a deal?" Madison asked.

The man blew out a long exhale, rustling the hairs on his beard. "I have information about Dolumhart. Isn't that the reason your sister died? She was going to rat them out?"

Madison leaned forward. "What do you know about her death and Dolumhart?"

"I drive their trucks across the border every week, bringing their tainted Morvecet in and out of Canada."

"How?" Tucker asked.

"They're disguising them in their other pain killers' bottles."

Wyatt sat at the table. "They're selling them already without approval?"

Brian popped forward, getting into Madison's space. "Until your sister ruined it for everyone."

Tucker jolted upward.

Madison raised her hand in a stop position. She didn't want him intervening. "What do you mean about Leah?"

"Just that she was a troublemaker."

"Who murdered her? Maybe Emerson will get you a deal if you help us bring her killer to justice." Not that she'd allow it, but she had to get him to talk.

"Now we're getting somewhere. I only know him as Cicada." He slouched. "Obviously, not his actual name."

Something niggled Madison about this man's story. What were they missing? She got up and paced around the small room. *Think, Madison, think.*

Wait—she stopped midstep and spun around to face the redhead. "If you drove their trucks every day, you should have known better than to use this crossing. Why did you want to get caught?"

His eyes widened.

Bingo.

He bit his lip, the cocky attitude dissipating.

Tucker hauled him from the chair. "Tell us the truth this time."

"He wanted you here." His whisper was barely audible.

He? Here?

A shudder rocked Madison, sending ice into her veins. "What do you mean?"

"Don't trust—"

Gunfire erupted somewhere in the building, cutting off Brian's warning.

Wyatt, Tucker and Madison all reached for their sidearms as the small room snapped into darkness.

Tucker reached for the Maglite on his duty belt and turned it on. Even though it was early morning, the windowless room plummeted into darkness with the sudden attack. Hairs prickled the back of his neck at Brian's words. *He wanted you here.* Whoever orchestrated this encounter went to extreme measures to make it happen. Purposely sending a driver to the wrong border crossing, knowing he would get caught. What was their endgame? To eliminate the task force picking up the investigation after Leah's death? Or were they targeting Madi alone?

He didn't want to wait to find out.

"He's gonna kill me too." Brian stood. "Help me and I'll tell you everything I know."

Tucker shone the light in the prisoner's direction. His wild eyes told Tucker he was both serious and scared. Clearly, the man hadn't expected to come under attack.

"Wyatt, we'll secure the building." He turned to Madi. "Stay here with Mr. Brown. We need to find a way out and escort him back into Canada."

She nodded and reholstered her weapon. "Mr. Brown, sit down. When it's safe, we'll leave."

The man's Adam's apple bounced as he gazed at each of them. "But, we need—"

"Do as the lady said, Mr. Brown." Wyatt called 911 and informed the operator of their situation. He stuffed his phone back into his pocket and opened the door a crack, then peeked out. "Hall is clear. Tucker, this way." He raised his Glock.

"Madison, be on alert." Tucker's tone commanded obedience.

She pressed her lips into a straight line. "Always."

Right. She knew how to do her job. Why had he assumed otherwise? Her safety was his first concern, and he had the sudden urge to pull her into a hug but now wasn't the right time. Plus, he never wanted to put himself back into her life again. Not after she'd ripped out his heart.

He held her gaze. *Lord, keep her safe.*

A small smile skittered across her gorgeous face.

He gave her a slight nod and followed Wyatt from the room. They both crouch-crawled down the hall in tight formation. The fact that this border-patrol agent knew how to proceed in an attack told Tucker he probably had military experience. What was his story?

Gunfire followed by shouts intermingled with cursing interrupted his thoughts, plunging him back into the moment.

"Where is she?" A voice boomed from around the corner.

Wyatt raised his fist in the air, indicating Tucker to freeze.

He stopped and held his breath.

"Who are you talking about?" a voice asked.

"The Canadian politician's other daughter."

Madi.

"Who?"

Shuffling footsteps sounded followed by a choking noise.

Tucker risked a glance and edged closer, gazing around the corner.

A masked man had a machine gun pressed at a female's temple and he held his hand at her throat. Another suspect stood off to the side, his weapon raised at a different officer.

Tucker scanned the outer office. There were only two. At least they were even in their ratio of perps to officers. That gave them more of an advantage.

"CBSA officer Madison Steele. We know she's here." The first man grabbed her collar and pushed the gun farther into her temple.

The woman shifted her gaze in their direction.

Tucker darted his head back.

Her simple gesture gave away their location. They had to move now. "Is there another way out of the building?" Tucker whispered.

Wyatt shook his head. "Only a window at the end of the hall, but you'll never make it out in time. Sally's given us away."

"John, check down that hall," the voice said.

"Move." Wyatt cemented his stance, bringing his weapon to eye level. "I'll distract them. You get Madison to safety."

Tucker nodded and put his hand on Wyatt's arm. "Stay safe."

"Madison Steele, we know you're here," the voice yelled. "Give yourself up and we might let you live. He just wants to talk."

He?

Was he referring to Daniel Levine of Dolum-hart? Or someone else?

Rushed footsteps sounded nearby.

"Go!" Wyatt's whisper spoke urgency.

Tucker bolted back to the room and opened the door. Sunlight from the window in the hall beamed into the small space.

Madi's raised gun greeted him.

"It's just me, Madi. We have to go. Now!"

"Tucker, I could have shot you."

Rustling sounded behind the door followed by a thud.

"They're coming. Wyatt is distracting them." He hauled Brian up and removed the cuffs. "Don't try anything."

"How will we get out?" Madi asked.

"There's a window at the end of the hall. It's our only option from here." He opened the door and checked the area.

A masked man lay on the floor with a knife protruding from his neck. His lifeless eyes confirmed his condition.

Wyatt pointed to the window and mouthed, "Go!"

One down. One to go.

"John?" The other suspect yelled from the front office. "What did you find?"

Silence.

They'd come looking for his partner. Time to run.

Tucker slid the window open and turned back to Wyatt, raising his eyebrows. They needed another distraction.

Wyatt nodded. He understood Tucker's intent. He raised his weapon and inched around the corner. "John isn't coming. Give it up, man. You're surrounded."

Sirens confirmed his statement.

Tucker took the distraction and pushed the screen

out. It thudded to the ground. He surveyed the drop and turned back. "Madi, it's not far. Ease yourself out feetfirst, jump and roll on landing."

She nodded and scrambled into position with her back to Tucker.

He wrapped his arms around her and lifted her through.

She jumped and rolled before righting herself and pulling out her weapon.

Tucker turned to Brian. "You're next."

He did the same for the prisoner and then eased himself through the window before jumping to safety.

Shots from the front of the building greeted them.

He pulled his Smith & Wesson from his holster. "Move. Now!"

They raced to his cruiser and secured Brian before hopping into the front seat.

"You okay?" he asked Madi as he put the vehicle in gear and raced out of the parking lot.

Madi brushed dirt from her jacket. "Yes. Is Wyatt?"

"I can tell he knows what he's doing. He'll be fine."

"He's ex-military."

"Figured as much."

Brian whimpered from the backseat.

So much for the cocky-attitude suspect from earlier. He'd realized someone had used him.

Madi grabbed Tucker's arm. "Wait. We need to search the Dolumhart truck first."

"No time. We'll get Wyatt to inspect it."

She slumped back into the seat. "Who were the assailants?"

"Only caught a first name. John. I doubt his real name. Hopefully, they can ID him from his fingerprints." He turned his head. "Brian, what else can you tell us about this gang and the one you called Cicada?"

They needed to get as much out of this man as soon as possible. This ruthless gang anticipated their every move. Somehow.

"I never met Cicada. Just heard of him and trust me. You don't want to mess with him." Brian's shaky voice revealed his fear.

Madi reached around and joggled her finger in the prisoner's direction. "What are you hiding? Why did you lure us to this station?"

Tucker glanced in the rearview mirror.

The man's eyes bulged.

"He only told me that Cicada needed you alive. You have something he wants."

What? Could someone else know about the flash drive? Or was he referring to Leah's laptop?

Tucker pulled on to the bridge that connected Calais to St. Stephen. The busy morning traffic made it impossible for him to get back to Canada quickly.

Madi's phone dinged and she fished it from her

pocket. "Wyatt. The other suspect got away, but the building is secure." She typed. "I'm telling him to tear the truck apart."

"Good. Glad he's safe. Seems like a good guy."

"He's a sweetheart."

Something in her voice raised his jealousy level.

Tucker, don't go there. Remember your possible condition.

He shook any romantic urges away and pulled in behind the line of stopped vehicles.

Flashing lights ahead caught his attention. "Something's going on."

"It's him." Brian's whispered voice could barely be heard as Tucker's radio crackled.

"Be on the lookout," Dispatch said. "Armed—"

An explosion rocked the bridge.

The pavement buckled, and the cruiser plummeted downward.

Toward the Saint Croix River.

Brian's scream boomed in Tucker's ear as regrets pressed upon Tucker. Would he live long enough to figure out his feelings for Madi?

The vehicle slammed into the water.

The air bags crashed into his face, plunging him into darkness.

EIGHT

Madison's erratic heartbeat matched the throbbing in her head as spots filled her vision through the murky water. Her weakened limbs immobilized her like a caterpillar wrapped in a cocoon. Would this be how she died? In a submerged coffin? All her life she feared dying and imagined what it would be like, but she wasn't ready. She had too much to do in this life. Too many regrets. Too many unresolved hurts. *God, help!* A phrase Brenda recently said popped into her mind.

God is in ALL things. Everywhere. You just need to know where to look.

Was God really there?

The explosion had caused the windows to fracture into spiderweb-like cracks, making it easier for the river to consume the interior of the cruiser. Tucker moaned as the water gushed higher. The icy substance jolted Madison, pumping adrenaline into her body. She had to act.

Fast.

Tucker needed her. It had only been seconds since they hit the river, but his unconscious state and the fast-filling grave would entomb him soon if she didn't act quickly.

She fumbled with the seat belt and fought to unfasten the mechanism. Finally, it snapped open.

Brian bumped the back passenger window with

his feet. He'd escape soon, but she'd sacrifice their prisoner to save Tucker.

More water gushed in as Brian busted his window and swam upward, chilling her to the bones.

Ignoring him, she reached over and tried Tucker's seat belt. It wouldn't budge. "Come on!" She tugged at the strap, but it held strong. *Think, Madison!* What would Tucker do if the roles were reversed?

She shook his shoulders. "Wake up!" Her muffled words bubbled as the water rose above chin level.

She gagged as panic threatened to drown her and she knew they would hit bottom in another few seconds. She needed to get them both to the surface.

Madison eyed Tucker's duty belt and noticed a multitool pocketknife beside his gun. She flipped the case open and pulled it out, releasing the blade. She mustered up courage as the water continued to rise, and sawed through the seat belt. She was running out of time.

You can do this! Seconds later, the blade cut through the belt, freeing Tucker.

How could she get him through the window and to the surface? The water would soon rise over their heads. Tucker would drown if she couldn't get them to safety. She turned in her seat and placed her boots on the window. She gathered strength and whacked her feet on it several times until the cracked window shattered.

She turned back to Tucker and encircled her arms around his chest, pulling him up and out of the driver's seat. Thankfully, the water created a buoyancy and made him feel lighter. She gulped in a huge breath and pulled them out the window. Kicking with all her strength, she swam upward with him in tow.

With increased adrenaline she made it to the surface within seconds, bursting out of the water and gulping in air.

"There they are!" someone from above yelled.

Pfht! Pfht!

Bullets slammed into the river beside them, spraying her in the face.

She gasped. Too close for comfort.

Madison glimpsed masked men aiming their weapons from the damaged bridge, making their intent clear.

The *he* Brian mentioned was still out to eliminate them.

Tucker stirred and opened his eyes.

"Big breath. We're going under again!" Madison hoped her words registered in his foggy brain.

She tightened her grip around Tucker, gulped in a huge breath, and dropped back under the surface.

It was their only hope of escape.

Tucker woke at the sudden jolt of icy waters. He held his breath. Where was he? Disorientated, he blinked and saw a bloodstained Brian sinking in the river beside him. He sensed his body against Madi's as she kicked downward. Why was she pulling them back under?

A bullet sliced through the river, answering his question.

They were under fire and it would be hard to escape with him adding his weight to hers as she struggled to get them to safety.

He pulled away from her and nodded.

She pointed to the right and he understood her intent.

Get to the closer Canadian shoreline as quickly as they could.

His tired limbs and pounding head made it difficult, but he kicked with all his strength. *God, protect us from the gunfire.*

More bullets blasted into the river.

His lungs were about to burst, but he swam faster.

A bullet slammed into the water beside Madi, hitting her shoulder. She stopped, stunned at the impact before grabbing her wound.

Tucker kicked harder and came up beside her. He gathered her into his arms and proceeded to the shoreline.

Suddenly, Madi's body went limp. The pain must have caused her to pass out. He needed to risk a surface break, or they'd never make it.

Tucker stopped and treaded water, glancing around.

No more bullets penetrated the river. Perhaps they were safe.

He swam upward. As he reached the surface, he edged his head and Madi's above water to gage their situation. He gulped in much-needed air.

Sirens blared as shouts screamed in the distance. Police officers and border-patrol agents scurried around cars on the portion of the bridge still intact. No masked men in sight.

"Tucker! You're almost to the shoreline. Keep going." Jenkins yelled from above before racing toward the river's edge.

After what seemed like an eternity, Tucker made it to the side and Jenkins helped pull them out of the water.

"She's. Been. Shot." Tucker's breathless words came out in spurts.

"Paramedics are en route," Jenkins said.

Tucker felt Madi's neck for a pulse.

Weak, but she wasn't breathing.

He began compressions.

Nothing.

"Come on, Madi!" He repeated the process as he prayed for God to save her.

After the third round, Madi coughed and water spewed from her mouth.

Tucker turned her sideways. "Thank You, God."

Madi grabbed her shoulder and breathed in and out.

"We made it, Madi. Paramedics are on their way."

"Brian?"

Sirens sounded nearby, and a crowd gathered on the shoreline. "Jenkins, can you move the crowd back so the paramedics can get through?"

Jenkins nodded and stretched his arms out. "Folks, give them room."

"They shot Brian, Madi. We'll need divers to pull his body out."

She eased herself up. "You okay?"

Tucker touched the goose egg on his forehead. "My head took a beating and other than being exhausted and cold, I'm fine. I'll get one of the paramedics to check it. Thank you for getting me out of the car. That probably wasn't easy."

"Definitely a challenge," Madi said. "Did they catch the shooters?"

"Don't know." He glanced toward the damage. "A team is moving the other passengers from the bridge, but it appears the explosion was right in front of our cruiser."

She winced. "Do you think they knew when we were right on top of the explosive device?"

"Yes. They were watching, but I think they're long gone now."

"Tucker!"

He turned to see Charlotte and Teddy making their way toward them.

Tucker waved the duo over. "Madi took a hit to the shoulder, but I think the bullet just grazed her."

Charlotte kneeled beside them. "You okay, handsome?"

Did she have to call him that all the time? He bit the inside of his mouth to stop himself from saying something he'd regret. "Just a small bump on my head. Please take care of Madi." He winced at the tone he knew he'd just conveyed, but he needed her to pay attention to Madi's wound.

"Let me see." Charlotte grabbed scissors and cut through Madi's jacket and uniform shirt before inspecting her shoulder. "Definitely a graze, but a deep one. You're gonna need stitches, love."

Madi sighed. Loudly. "I hate needles."

Teddy grabbed a bandage. "Well, you're gonna have to suck it up, princess."

"Have some compassion, man." Tucker cringed at this paramedic's negativity.

Teddy waggled a gloved finger toward Tucker. "Stay out of it, Constable." He laced the word constable with sarcasm. He turned back to Madi. "We need to take you to the hospital."

She bit her lip.

A nervous habit he adored, but he could tell her anxiety level just elevated a notch. He rubbed her arm. "I'll be with you. Don't worry."

Charlotte clucked her tongue. "No, you won't. Family only."

What was in her tone? Anger? Resentment?

"Let's go, Madison." Charlotte stood and helped Teddy get Madi on a gurney.

Jenkins stumbled through the long grass. "Tucker, what do you want me to do with the scene?"

Tucker rubbed his brow. "Call Hyatt and request more officers. Secure the area and get divers to recover our prisoner's body. Identified himself as Brian Brown at the Calais border, but we're not sure it's his actual name. Look into that." He paused. "Oh, we'll need new cells and equipment. Ours are waterlogged. Check with Madison's superintendent."

"On it." He pulled out his radio and ran back up the embankment.

Assured they would contain the scene, Tucker joined Madi in the ambulance despite Charlotte's objection. The paramedic inspected his goose egg as they raced to Charlotte County Hospital.

Once they arrived, Tucker jumped from the vehicle as another ambulance pulled beside them.

The paramedics removed a gurney from the back and Tucker caught a glimpse of the woman being rushed inside.

"Mom?"

"Someone was looking out after you, young lady," the doctor said after stitching Madison's wound.

Was it true? Had God really helped them escape a submerged tomb?

Brenda would agree with the doctor's assessment, and while Madison was thankful they survived, her stubborn attitude wouldn't concede submission to an unseen entity. Not yet.

Especially after all the pain He'd allowed in her life.

What happened with Tucker's mother? The paramedics rushed her into the hospital, and Tucker followed after Madison assured him she'd be okay.

Would his mom end up like Dolly?

She smoothed out her now dry uniform pants. It had been almost two hours since Tucker pulled her from the river, and even though she was no longer wet, the grunginess lingered. "Am I free to go, Doc?"

"Yes, but take it easy for the rest of the day." He removed his gloves and opened the curtain.

Like that would happen. They had a case to solve.

"Thanks for your help," she said.

He made a note on her chart. "Take pain killers for any discomfort."

Hardly. Not after what this case unearthed. Tainted drugs. Murder. Conspiracy.

No way.

She exited the room and rounded the corner to look for Tucker when she collided with her boss. "Sir, what are you doing here?"

"Checking on you." Sam Watson's gruff voice didn't hide the compassion.

She knew that even though her boss was hard on her at times, he still cared for those under his watch.

"And to give you these." He handed her a cell phone and another Beretta.

"Appreciate it." She rubbed her shoulder.

"You okay? You don't look so good."

Almost drowning and getting shot will do that to you. The thought lingered in her mind, but she held her tongue. She needed to ditch her foul mood and concentrate on catching whoever targeted them.

She pasted on a smile. "I'm fine. Did you hear from Wyatt about the attack at their station?"

"Yes, he called after the explosion to check on you and Tucker. The second attacker got away."

"How? The police arrived as we left."

"They had help."

Madison stuffed the new cell phone into her pocket and the weapon into the back of her pants. "What do you mean?"

"Someone diverted the police to a rear entrance, so the suspect could sail out the front. Free and clear."

"Do you think a border-patrol agent assisted them?" She knew anything was possible.

"Police are interrogating everyone, so hopefully we'll get new information soon," Sam said.

"Have they identified the dead assailant?"

"They're running his prints. If he has a record, they'll find out who he is."

"We need a break." Madison fingered her damp

braid. A reminder of her near-death experience. A question lingered. Who wanted her dead?

Sam grabbed her arm. "Listen, why didn't you tell me you had a sister and that it was Emerson Peters's daughter?"

Why hadn't she?

"It never came up."

Sam's eyes narrowed and he squeezed her arm. "Don't trust that man."

She suppressed a gasp at his quick change of demeanor. "What are you worried about, Superintendent Watson?"

His eyes softened. "You."

Why?

"Don't worry—I'll be fine. Tucker will protect me."

He released his grip. "I hope so. We can't lose you." He cleared his throat. "You're a valuable employee."

Why was her boss so touchy-feely all of a sudden? Was it because she almost died today?

Or something else?

She set the question aside. "Have the divers found Brian yet?"

"Oddly enough, no."

Why did that not surprise her? "They need to widen their search."

"They have. I'll keep you updated." His cell phone dinged and he glanced at the screen. Once again his eyes narrowed. "Gotta run. Keep me apprised of your investigation." He stomped down the hall.

After locating Beverley Reed's room, Madison plunked herself into a chair in the corner to wait for Tucker to talk to the doctor. She eyed his mother's ashen face. Had the Morvecet claimed another victim?

Madison gripped the armrests tighter. This had to stop.

Now.

Tucker rushed into the room.

She jumped up at his abrupt entrance. "What's wrong?"

He held out his cell phone. "Just got a text from Jenkins. We need to get to Dolumhart now. He's already on his way there."

"Why?"

"An employee called the station stating they want to pick up where Leah left off."

"Who?"

Tucker stuffed his phone back into his pocket. "Don't know. The call dropped before they gave their name."

Could this be the break they were waiting for?

She glanced back at Beverley. Was it Madison's imagination, or had the woman grown even whiter? "What about your mom?"

"Doc said it's a wait-and-see situation. We need to find this gang."

And they were running out of precious time.

Tucker's mother would pay the price if they didn't solve this mystery.

Now.

NINE

Tucker followed Madi into Dolumhart Pharmaceuticals with a heaviness overtaking his already weary body. He forced his feet to take each step. Even though they had dried out from their plunge into the water, he longed to change his clothes, but there wasn't time. The frantic call from the employee had propelled them back into action. Plus, his mother's condition had worsened. The doctor hadn't given Tucker much hope. Not without some sort of antidote to counteract the Morvecet. If that was even possible. *God, give us wisdom to stop these criminals before—*

He swallowed a lump of emotion. He couldn't go there. The thought of losing his mother paralyzed him and threatened to block him in his tracks. He prayed for strength and protection for Madi and his team. And healing for his mother.

Hyatt had dropped off another vehicle for them and emphasized the need to get to the bottom of this threat. Like Tucker needed reminding of what was at stake.

Tucker's phone rang. Emerson. *Great, I don't need his pressure too.* However, if he ignored the man, he'd never hear the end of it. He hit the Answer button. "Mr. Peters, what can I do for you?"

Madi halted and turned, raising a brow.

Tucker shrugged at her unspoken question.

"What are you doing to find my daughter's killer?" Emerson's abrupt tone boomed in Tucker's ear.

I don't need your attitude. Not after what we've been through already today. "Following up on a lead, sir."

"Good. You need to finish this or I'll have your badge."

Tucker gripped his cell phone tighter. He wasn't about to take this man's attitude. "With all due respect, sir, I almost drowned today and was also shot at. I don't need you threatening to get me fired."

Madi shook her head.

Emerson swore. "I'm sorry. Are you okay?"

"Fine. Will you let me do my job?"

"Of course."

Tucker's shoulders drooped. If the polls proved true, he'd just been rude to the province's next premier. "Listen, I'm sorry. I'm just on edge. I realize you want answers to Leah's death."

"I have no right to take my frustration out on you. I heard your mother was sick. I'll say a prayer for her."

How did he find that out? Tucker knew he had well-placed connections, but his mother was just hospitalized. "Thank you. I'll keep you informed of what I can."

"You do that. Stay safe." The politician clicked off.

"What did he want?" Madison asked.

"An update on who killed Leah."

"He needs to stay out of it and let us do our job."

"Why do you dislike him so much?"

Madi wrinkled her nose. "Just something about him rubs me the wrong way, I guess."

"He's your stepfather and now the only family you have left."

"I have Bren."

"You know what I mean. Are you sure you're okay to do this?"

Madi rubbed her shoulder. "I'm fine."

He gestured toward the elevators. "Let's go."

Jenkins greeted them in the foyer of the plush offices. "What took you so long?"

Tucker could do without this man's nastiness. However, he'd ignore his disposition for now. They had a job to do. "What do you have?"

"Daniel Levine is stonewalling us."

"Of course he is." Tucker approached the vice president's office, bypassing the flirtatious Annabelle. He didn't have time for her.

She jumped up. "Constable, you can't go in there."

He avoided her gaze and opened Levine's door. "Sir, we need to speak to your staff."

The man bolted upright. "You can't just barge in here. Do you have a warrant this time?"

Madi stepped around Tucker. "What are you hiding?"

Levine's eyes widened. "You again. I don't have

time for this. Security will escort you out." He picked up his phone.

Tucker rushed across the room and pushed the button to end the call. "Did I mention I'm friends with Emerson Peters? Do I need to get *him* to call *you*?"

He wouldn't be intimidated and wasn't afraid to pull the politician-connection card. Not with his mother's and Madi's lives on the line.

Levine fiddled with his bright yellow tie before plopping back into his leather chair. "Fine. What do you need?"

"Access to your employee list, so we can interview them," Tucker said. "Prove to us you have nothing to hide."

Madi harrumphed behind him.

She didn't trust the man and who could blame her? Someone within this organization murdered her sister and had tainted drugs smuggled across the border into Maine. Drugs that killed.

Once again, Levine lifted his receiver and pushed a button. "Bella, give the officers a list of our employees, would you, dear?"

Tucker cringed at the familiarity of his tone with his receptionist. What other secrets lurked in the corners of Dolumhart Pharmaceuticals?

Levine slammed the phone back into its cradle. "Done. Now, get out of my office."

Gladly.

Tucker followed Madi and Jenkins back into the foyer.

"Nicely done," Jenkins said. "I guess being friends with a politician pays off." His words didn't match the sarcasm in his voice.

Jenkins still concluded Emerson got Tucker his promotion.

Did Hyatt and the rest of the St. Stephen force think that too?

He couldn't dwell on his teammates now and approached Annabelle's desk. "Do you have the employee list?"

She grabbed a piece of paper from the printer and handed it to him. "Here you go, but you won't find anything. We're a family here at Dolumhart and family sticks together."

What did that mean?

He'd ignore that for now. He took the list. "Thank you. Where are these individuals located?"

She pointed to the right of her desk. "Go through there and you'll find everyone. I've informed the group you're coming."

Madi opened the glass door. "Is there an office to interview people?"

Annabelle flattened her lips. "Yes, a boardroom across from the cubicles. It's empty right now. There's also an office too that you can use."

"Thanks, Bella," Jenkins said.

Tucker didn't miss the man's wink in her direction. Really? He grabbed the officer's arm. "That was unprofessional and uncalled for."

"Why don't you tattle on me with Emerson?" Jenkins sailed past Madi and stomped down the corridor.

"What's his problem?" Madi asked.

"Who knows? He doesn't like me." He glanced at the list. "We need to divide and conquer."

"But we're better interrogating together."

They had always played well off each other, but would he admit that he wanted nothing more than to be at her side all the time? Especially with her life at risk. His protective nature wanted to ensure nothing happened to her. "Let's split the names with Jenkins." He folded the paper and ripped it in half.

"But how will we learn which employee called your station? They didn't give a name, right?"

Tucker rubbed his neck. The day had already been taxing, and it was only noon. "No, the call dropped before they could identify themselves. It was a male though, according to Jenkins."

"Let's start with them."

They spent an hour interrogating all the males on their list but one. Cal Perkins. None of the others claimed to know of any tainted drugs within their company. Tucker could tell from reading their body language that most were telling the truth. Others…not so much.

A knock sounded.

"Come in," Tucker said. "Cal Perkins?"

The bald, thirtysomething-year-old nodded. He sat and templed his fingers. "What can I do for you, officers? Am I in trouble?"

"Why would you think that?" Tucker asked.

"Well, it's not every day the police come to talk to you at your place of employment." He shifted his glance from one to the other. "Especially one who's friends with a high-ranking politician."

Tucker stood and leaned against a wall, crossing his arms. His stance personified authority. "And how would you know that information, Mr. Perkins?"

"Doesn't everyone?" He sat back and crossed his arms, matching Tucker's authoritative position.

Just what game was this man playing? They had to regain control of the conversation.

Madi leaned forward. "Mr. Perkins, whether Constable Reed is friends with Mr. Peters is irrelevant to this interview. Can you tell me if you worked closely with Mr. Peters's daughter?"

Cal swallowed before his lips tightened.

Why the disgust over the mention of Leah's name? Tucker needed to probe deeper. "You didn't like her?"

"No." He turned to Madi. "Your sister was a troublemaker."

Tucker's suspicion rose a notch. This man knew too much about them.

"Why would you say that?" Madi stood and fingered a picture on the wall.

"She wouldn't stop her relentless pursuit of dragging the company through the mud."

Tucker circled the long boardroom table. "Wasn't she just trying to understand the Morvecet test results? Lives are at stake."

The man slammed his hand on the table. "She didn't know what she was talking about!" His nostrils flared. "It was because of her we had to go through additional clinical phases."

Something about his demeanor just didn't sit right with Tucker. He was putting on a good show, but was he really that oblivious to what was happening at Dolumhart?

Madi turned. "But your company still went ahead even after doctored results."

The man's mouth dropped open. "What are you talking about? Your sister made this up. Mr. Levine copied us on the email stating we weren't going to market yet."

"Do you really believe that?" Madi asked.

"That's what management told us. Leah's information was wrong."

Poker face. The man was a good liar, or he clearly accepted Dolumhart's claim. What else had Daniel Levine hidden from his staff? Was he responsible for Leah's death?

Madi sat and tapped her thumb on the mahogany

table. "My sister would not make this allegation if it wasn't true."

He sneered. "How well did you really know your sister, Officer Steele?"

Tucker rubbed his temple, trying to ward off a tension headache. Or perhaps he was just tired of this man's attitude.

Madi spread her hands out on the table. "What does that mean?" Her voice betrayed both hurt and anger.

Tucker moved next to her and placed his hand on her shoulder, giving her a cue to rein in her emotions. "Mr. Perkins, what do you do at Dolumhart?" He glanced at the employee list. "Says here you're management. Of what?"

"The accounting department," Cal said.

Tucker studied the man's face. He couldn't be any older than early thirties. How did he become a manager at so young an age? Once again, Tucker's attention piqued.

"Have you noticed anything unsettling in the finances?" Tucker sat beside Madi.

"Should I?"

Tucker wrote in his notebook. "Your profits remained the same?"

"They're solid."

Madi circled her finger on the table. "If they hadn't gone to production, wouldn't the company's profits have fluctuated?"

Cal Perkins flinched. "I… I don't…know what

you're talking about." His words came out stuttered, his previous composed demeanor gone.

They had him. This manager had information and was hiding it.

"You're lying, Mr. Perkins." Tucker leaned forward. "Tell us what you know about Morvecet."

"I told you. Nothing." He stood. "If that's all. I have a department to run."

"Sit down." Tucker's authoritative voice spoke volumes. He wasn't finished with this man yet.

Cal obeyed.

"Did you have something to do with Leah Peters's death?" Tucker asked.

The manager's eyes bulged. "What? No!"

"But you didn't like her very much and thought she was getting in the way," Madi said.

"It's no secret we didn't get along, but I wouldn't harm her." He looked left.

"But…?" Tucker guessed he was evading the truth.

Cal snapped his focus back to them. "Understand, if it comes out, I'm fired."

"If what comes out?" Tucker asked. "My team is talking to many employees today. We will not divulge the source of any information we receive."

The man twirled his university ring. "Mr. Levine and Annabelle are having an affair. Leah threatened to expose them. Mr. Levine is married and highly involved in large nonprofit organizations.

If it got out he was cheating on his wife, it would ruin his reputation."

"And they would pull any funding." Madi's face blanched, revealing her disgust for the VP loud and clear.

"Exactly. Understand me, I did not hurt Leah."

"But you suspect Mr. Levine and Annabelle?" Tucker asked.

The man sighed loudly. "I don't know what to believe."

"One more question." Tucker tapped his pen. "Did you call the police detachment earlier this morning?"

"No. Why would I? I don't want to lose my job."

"Thank you for your time." Tucker stood. "We'll be in touch if we need any further information."

Cal nodded and shuffled out of the room.

"We need to have a conversation with Annabelle," Madi said. "She's definitely not as sweet as she's portraying."

"Agreed. There's something else going on in this office and we need to understand it."

But the question remained—who had so much to hide that they would risk murder?

A text chimed.

He swiped the screen. Hyatt.

Tox report shows Dolly died from a strong dosage of fentanyl given instead of morphine at hair salon.

What?

They needed to talk to Charlotte and Teddy.

This had to have been a mistake. No way would a paramedic mix up those drugs.

This case just got even more disturbing.

Madison noted Tucker's slumped shoulders and tightened lips. She grabbed his arm. "What is it?"

He pushed his cell phone across the table. "Read this."

She gazed at the words. "What? How could seasoned paramedics mess these two drugs up?" Charlotte was a flirt and annoying, but she gave no indication of being careless. Teddy on the other hand was a ticking time bomb, ready to explode at a moment's notice.

Tucker ran his fingers through his knotted brown hair. "We have to talk to them, but we need to finish here first. Let's chat with Annabelle, shall we?"

Ten minutes later, the receptionist sat across the table biting her bright yellow nails. Her agitated state told Madison the young woman was worried about something.

"Annabelle, you didn't include yourself on the list of employees you gave me," Tucker said. "Why?"

"I'm only the receptionist. What information would I have?" She scratched at her neck before fiddling with her pendant.

She definitely had information. But, what? Evidence of an affair?

"Start by telling us your last name," Madison said. "It's not on your nameplate."

"Atkins."

Tucker leaned forward. "As in Teddy Atkins's kid sister?"

She glanced away, but not before Madison caught the twisted look of disgust on her face. Was she ashamed of Teddy? Or was it more complicated?

"Yes," she whispered. "He won't admit it though."

"Why is that?" Tucker asked.

"He hates me for what I did."

Was she admitting to the affair that easily? Madison didn't believe she'd give up information without some persuasion. "What did you do, Annabelle?"

She returned her gaze back to Madison, her eyes flashing hatred their way. "Isn't that why you called me in here? Someone ratted me out."

Tucker clasped his hands into a tented position. "How about you be more specific?"

"Your sister found out about Daniel and me." She rubbed a fallen tear away. "She was going to tell everyone."

"So, it's true then. You were having an affair?" Madison asked.

She nodded, biting her lip.

"Why, Annabelle?" Tucker stood and circled around the table, sitting in the chair next to her. "You have everything going for you. He's got to be twenty-five years your senior."

"That's what Teddy said too."

"How long has it been going on?" Not that Madison wanted details, but it could be a key to her sister's murder.

"It started a year ago as a dare from someone in the organization. They said I'd never move up in the company if I didn't get close to him." Another tear escaped. "Then I tried to stop it after Teddy found out. He warned me that no one could find out about it, so I told Daniel we were through."

"Let me guess," Tucker said. "He wouldn't let you and held it over your head?"

Annabelle pulled up her long-sleeved shirt and exposed multiple bruises.

Madison slouched back in her chair.

This proved Daniel Levine was violent.

Did he also order the hit on Leah?

A wave of quivers raced through Madison, sending her pulse galloping.

Tucker squeezed Annabelle's shoulder. "I have to report him. He can't get away with this."

"No!" She bolted out of her chair. "He'll kill me. He's already—"

She plunked herself back down and clamped her mouth shut.

"Already what?" Madison asked. "Did he put the hit on my sister, Annabelle?"

"Not sure. Leah threatened to go public with our affair, so nothing would surprise me with that monster." She almost spat her words out.

Madison moved to the other side of the young

woman and placed her hands over top of Annabelle's. "Tell us what you can about what's going on at Dolumhart. You're the receptionist. You must have seen something."

She pulled away, biting her fluorescent orange lips once again.

"You can trust us," Tucker said. "We'll protect you. Let's put him away."

"He'll know." Annabelle stood and walked to the door, holding its handle. "This is why I called the police this morning."

Tucker stood. "It was you? We were told it was a male."

"I disguised my voice. I'm good at accents and impersonations. Almost went into acting." She raised her chin, determination returning to the earlier skittish young woman. "I'll leave you with this information. Interview Andy Richards." She walked out of the room.

Tucker fell back into his chair.

Madison grabbed his arm. "Isn't Andy your best friend from high school?"

"Yes. I didn't realize he worked here."

Why would Annabelle name him? Tucker and Andy were close in high school, but Madison had lost track of Andy. "He's not on the list?"

Tucker grabbed the paper. "He must be on the other half I tore off. Let me text Jenkins." He pulled out his cell phone and tapped a message. "Let's see what he has to say."

Moments later, the door opened and a scruffy-bearded, gaunt man entered with Jenkins.

Madison glanced at Tucker.

His widened eyes revealed his obvious surprise at his friend's appearance. Andy had always bragged about his muscles and was big into bodybuilding. What had happened?

And what did he know about her sister's death?

Tucker suppressed a sigh and dug his nails into his palms. Why had he not tried harder to stay in touch with Andy? The last Tucker heard was his friend had moved away to pursue a career somewhere in the States. No one seemed to know where.

Tucker stood and stretched out his hand. "Andy. It's been a long time. How are you?"

Andy stuffed his hands in his pockets, ignoring the gesture. "Why am I here?"

Jenkins nudged him forward. "Have a seat, Mr. Richards."

Andy plopped himself down. "I already told you. I know nothing."

Tucker scratched his head and sat in the seat across from his friend. "Andy, what do you do at Dolumhart?" Catching up with him needed to wait.

"Software developer." Andy tugged at his beard.

Tucker wrote the occupation in his notebook beside Andy's name. "For how long?"

"Two years now."

"Is that when you returned to St. Stephen?" Jenkins asked.

"Yup."

Wow. The chatterbox friend from high school now only offered a few words at a time.

Madi leaned back. "Andy, why haven't I seen you around town? You used to be so active with your peers. You barely even acknowledged your best friend here."

A question Tucker also wanted answered. Plus many more.

Andy moved his gaze to Tucker before peering at the table in front of him.

Why wouldn't he talk to him? Had Tucker offended his old friend?

"I can't say anything. He'll know." Andy looked at Jenkins before peering back down at his hands in his lap.

Did Jenkins make him nervous? Tucker had to gain control of the situation. Andy had information. "Jenkins, can we have the room?"

The officer stared, his eyes narrowing.

He didn't like Tucker giving him orders, but it couldn't be helped. They needed answers and something about his presence made Andy clam up.

Jenkins grunted and walked out of the room.

This interview better yield some results or his fellow officer would bad-mouth Tucker to Hyatt. They already had it in for him.

"Andy, tell us what's going on. You can trust us."

"So, the dynamic duo is back together again?" Andy's words held bitterness.

"Did I do something to offend you?" Tucker put his pen down and folded his hands. "What happened to you?"

The man slunk back in his chair. "Long story."

"We have time," Madi said. "You moved to the States?"

"Yes. I excelled in computer skills and gave up the idea of being a bodybuilder." He peered at Tucker. "I saw the way you looked at me earlier. You're disappointed, just like I suspected you'd be. You went to police college and excelled in law enforcement. All I did was play with computers."

Had Tucker been that bad of an influence that his friend thought he took stake in physical appearances or what he did for a living? "Not at all. Just surprised. You were so enthusiastic about pumping iron—I was just a bit shocked." He leaned forward. "Andy, I don't put stock in a person's vocation. We're all equal in God's eyes."

His friend's lip quivered.

Tucker was getting through to him. "Tell us what's going on."

"I got a job in California working for a computer company. I even moved my mother out with me as I was doing so well." He stood and paced. "But then I did something stupid that got me fired."

"What?" Madi asked.

Andy stopped pacing and gripped the back of a

leather chair. "I hacked into private information. Found out some terrible things and threatened to go public with it."

"What things?" Tucker asked.

"Embezzlement. Felt it was my duty to report it." He shoved the chair into a corner. It thudded against the wall, shaking the picture above it. Andy leveled the frame. "Never will do that again."

"Is that why you're being tight-lipped about what's going on around here?" Madi asked.

He turned, his eyes clouding. "They've threatened my family, man."

Tucker sucked in a breath and clenched his fists. "What? Who?"

Andy looked into the corner above their heads. He sat back down and grabbed Tucker's notebook, scribbling something. He shoved it closer to them.

They have eyes and ears everywhere.

It was then Tucker noticed the tiny camera lens in the corner ceiling. How had he missed it before?

That meant whoever *they* were also heard their conversation with Annabelle.

Now they were all in danger.

TEN

Madison sat in the small vacant office Andy brought them to after revealing the camera in the boardroom. He'd reassured Tucker and Madison that it didn't contain any video or listening devices. He'd done a sweep. They also found out from Jenkins that his interviews had been unsuccessful in obtaining any useful information. Everyone, including lower-level management, was tight-lipped about sharing what they knew concerning Morvecet. Jenkins left to inspect the files from the flash drive Madison had received from her sister. She hoped fresh eyes on it would help find something useful. She also needed to head to her sister's townhouse soon to follow up on her cryptic note regarding more evidence. For now, they waited for Andy to share information.

Madison glanced at Tucker's best friend. He sat in a nearby chair, his right knee bouncing. Something agitated him and it was essential they find out what.

"Andy, are you sure this room isn't bugged?" Tucker asked.

The man's gazed darted around the room. "Yes. I'm knowledgeable regarding surveillance equipment and ensure it isn't."

"Where did you learn to do that?" Madison removed her notebook and pen.

"You'd be surprised what the internet can tell you. Just had to research and order equipment."

"Okay, tell us what you know." Tucker stood against the wall with his arms folded, his brow wrinkled.

It appeared the constable had suspicions about his friend. After all, it had been years since they'd seen or talked to one another.

"Promise me you will keep my name out of any reports or news conferences. My family's lives depend on it." Andy's whispered words held urgency.

"We will," Tucker said. "Start at the beginning and leave nothing out."

Andy let out a long sigh. "You don't know this, but I have a daughter. I met a woman when I moved to California. We fell in love, got married and had Zoey." His lip quivered.

Madison touched his arm. "What is it, Andy?"

"Marcy died from complications during childbirth. I was a father and widower within minutes of each other. I'll never forget that day. It's etched into my brain forever." He leaned forward, elbows on his knees. "I took her death hard. Started drinking and gambling. My mother moved in with us to help look after Zoey. Couldn't have done it without her."

Tucker put his hand on Andy's shoulder. "Bud, I'm so sorry you went through that. I wish you would have contacted me."

Andy shook his head. "I don't know why I never told you where I was. Ashamed, I guess."

"Why?"

"Because I didn't amount to much in my career when you did."

Tucker pursed his lips. "Like I said, jobs don't make a man, Andy." He pointed to his friend's chest. "It's what's in there that counts."

"I understand that now. Anyway, I found myself at the casinos almost every night and squandered away any savings I'd built, so I had to find a way to make money to support my daughter. She was born with a heart condition and needed surgery at six months old."

"How old is she now?" Tucker asked.

"Seven."

Madison clutched the armrest. This man's grief still radiated from his body language years after losing his wife. She understood what it was like to have someone she loved robbed away, but his situation was entirely different. "What happened?"

"It was a few months after that I discovered my boss was embezzling funds from the company. I'm good at hacking into records." He threw his hands up. "I realize it's not a worthy trait, but I just started looking one day. Not sure why. Desperate perhaps. Anyway, once I found the information, I came up with a scheme to blackmail him for money. Money I needed to pay Zoey's hospital bills. To make a long story short, it backfired. He dismissed me and put the word out that I wasn't a reliable employee. I couldn't find work."

"Is that when you moved back here?" Tucker asked.

"No, my mother got a job to help and I stayed home to look after Zoey. Her condition improved after the surgery, thankfully."

Madison made a note. "What brought you back to St. Stephen?"

"Mom's brother was diagnosed with cancer and she wanted to be close to him." He paused. "I immediately got the job here. Not sure how I did, but they didn't seem to care that my previous company fired me. I started creating online applications for them. Then, out of the blue, I got a call from someone telling me they had my mother and Zoey."

Tucker plunked himself into a chair. "What? Who?"

"Not sure. The voice was distorted. They told me they wouldn't hurt my family if I cooperated."

"When was this?" Madison asked.

"Yesterday."

Madison froze. Just after Leah's email to the CEO and her death. "What did they want you to do?" They needed to question Brechin Cross, CEO of Dolumhart.

"Doctor all the test results of Morvecet and permanently remove a bunch of files."

Tucker whistled. "Why would they ask you?"

"Because they'd been in contact with my former boss. He apparently told them they fired me after I hacked into their system. The man said it was my computer skills that got me the job at Dolumhart and that I could remove the files without causing suspicion."

"They hired you because they recognized they may need your hacking capabilities one day." Tucker shook his head. "Unbelievable. Why didn't you go to the police?"

"They told me they were watching and would know if I did."

"And your family? Where are they now?" Madison asked.

"After I covered up their files, they released them back to me with a stern warning." Andy feverishly scratched his palm, turning it red. "Tell anyone and my family disappears. Forever this time."

"So why tell us now?" Tucker once again stood and peered out the window.

"Because people are dying from this drug. They need to be stopped."

Tucker turned. "But how? You removed the files, didn't you?"

"Yes."

Wait. How did Leah get the documents if he had removed them? "My sister had evidence against the company. When we showed some of it to Daniel Levine yesterday, he said he has no record of them. When were they deleted?"

"Yesterday morning. I made it look like a power surge."

"But we still have Leah's files," Madison said. "We can prove they're lying."

Andy got up and opened the door, peered out before closing it again. He pulled his chair close to Madison's and beckoned Tucker to his side. "I can too. I built a back door to retrieve them again." His whispered voice revealed his terrified state.

Madison's neck muscles released, hopefulness filling her mind. Could this be the break they needed? Would these files help corroborate and confirm what Leah left them? Maybe they could find more damaging evidence on Dolumhart's computers. Were they close to bringing this company to its knees and solving her sister's murder?

Tucker and Madison's cell phones dinged—simultaneously.

Tension inched back into her neck as she guessed the interruption only meant one thing.

Something terrible happened.

Tucker's pulse ricocheted at what news the collective text would reveal. The fact it went to both of them told him it wouldn't be good. He pulled out his cell phone and read. Hyatt. He'd sent it to the task force and Madi's superintendent.

We now have linked five deaths to Morvecet. Solve this case before any more happen. Emerson Peters has been calling for constant updates, threatening to pull any police funding if his daughter's murderer isn't found. Counting on you all, especially you, Constable Reed.

Of course his boss would single Tucker out. Jenkins was the corporal's favorite.

Tucker needed to enlist Andy's help. Now. Before they lost more lives. "Andy, we just received word that Morvecet has killed five more people. Will you help us?"

His friend's eyes widened before turning his gaze to the floor. "They'll kill my family."

"We'll protect you."

The man bolted out of his chair and stepped to the window. "No! I've changed my mind. I've told you too much already."

Madi stood beside the frightened man and grabbed his arm. "Andy, I understand your hesitancy, but they killed my sister. I need to find out who did it and bring them to justice. She didn't ask for this, but wouldn't let the public down by hiding what she uncovered. Can't you do the same?"

Madi's compassion touched Tucker, tugging at his heart. Her love for her sister shone through her eyes and actions. She'd turned into an amazing woman and one he could see himself dating.

If only his situation was different.

He shook off thoughts of love and raised his cell phone. "I'll contact my boss and get you 24-7 protection. I promise your mother and Zoey will be safe."

Could he really make such a promise? Exactly what would his boss offer?

Andy's shoulders slumped. "I'm so scared of losing them."

Tucker stood. "I get it, man. Family means everything. My mom is everything to me too, but guess where she is right now?"

"Where?"

"In the hospital because of Morvecet. She took it to ease her back pain and now the side effects are depleting the life—" He choked on his words. A sudden wave of fear passed over him and he had to sit. He'd just blown the tough-cop image he tried to portray, but the idea of losing his mother overwhelmed him. *God, what are You doing? Help us end this.* Confusion over why God would allow this in his life disturbed him. Hadn't he served Him wholeheartedly?

Andy sat beside him and squeezed Tucker's shoulder. "I'm sorry. Okay. I'll help, but you need to arrange my family's protection before I do anything. Those are my terms."

Tucker compartmentalized his mother's condition and his sudden anger at God. He needed to rein in his fears, especially when on the job. He prided himself in being professional and his reaction earlier was definitely not. *Get a grip, Tucker.*

"I'll call my superior right now." Annabelle's words from her interview rushed to his mind. He needed to get her protection too.

Wait—how did she know about Andy's involvement? Tucker definitely needed to chat with her again. There was more to her story.

Five minutes later after securing a plan with Hyatt regarding Andy and his family, he hung up. "Okay, we'll move all three of you to a safe house outside the town's limits. Are you willing to testify against Dolumhart and provide the evidence we need to put them away?"

He bit his lower lip. "I am."

"Okay, first we need to do this the right way and get a warrant. I don't want the company's lawyers coming back on us saying we didn't obtain this information correctly."

"How long will that take?" Madi asked. "We need to get the files and then put Andy into protective custody. Today."

"Perhaps Emerson can help."

"Do you think we'll find more than what we have from Leah's flash drive?" Madi asked.

Andy cleared his throat. "Leah didn't have everything. There's more hidden in the backdoor files. I just need my laptop to show you."

Hope surged through Tucker. Maybe they were close to finding who was behind this.

He stood and turned to Madi. "I need to make this call outside. You go with Andy discreetly and get his laptop. Don't leave his side. Then come back here. Since we don't know what other rooms have cameras, we need to use this space. Got it?"

She nodded.

Andy's eyes bulged.

Tucker could almost read his friend's fearful thoughts. "Madi is well trained and can protect you. Don't worry. I won't be long." He opened the door but hesitated. "Be careful and don't trust anyone."

Tucker resisted the urge to race through the corridors. He had to act normal and not create suspicion. They didn't know how many other employees had been coerced into helping those responsible.

Thankfully, Annabelle wasn't at her desk and he slipped by everyone without having to answer questions.

Moments later, he rushed out the building's front door. The crisp fall air sliced through his light jacket. He ignored the chill and pulled out his cell phone, punching in Emerson's number.

"Tucker, you have news?"

Straight to business. "Yes, but I can't go into specifics. I need your help. This could break open the case."

"Anything to help solve Leah's murder. My daughter was everything to me." The quiver in his voice revealed his deep grief.

"I need you to expedite a warrant from Judge Saunders. I'm going to call him now and give him specifics. I'll text you when I'm done. Once you hear from me, can you call him?"

"Absolutely. Saunders and I go way back and he owes me for helping him get into office."

"Thank you." An idea rose. "When are you having Leah's service?"

"Tomorrow. Will you be there?"

Suspects often attend funerals of those they'd murdered, so he'd plan on it. "Yes. Please let us know the details."

Silence.

A cardinal chirped in the distance, reminding him of peacefulness. However, these times were anything but peaceful. "Sir, you still there?"

"How is Madison doing?"

"Hanging on. She's devastated by Leah's death. Perhaps you should call her."

Once again, silence stilled the airway.

What was Emerson's hesitation with Madi? "Just a thought."

"I'll think about it. Gotta run. I'll call Saunders after you text me." He clicked off.

Five minutes later after speaking with the judge, Tucker sent Emerson a message. His help would allow them to get to the hidden files quicker.

He headed back to the building's entrance, but his cell phone buzzed and stopped him. He peered at the screen. Hyatt. Great. His calls were never good news.

He clicked Answer. "Reed here."

"Constable, didn't you give Leah's flash drive to Forensics?"

"Yesterday. Why?"

"Jenkins tried to retrieve it from them. It's gone."

Tucker's neck muscles tightened. "What? Are you sure?"

"It's not there."

"Good thing I took a copy." Tucker opened the building's front door and stepped inside the lobby.

"Where is it?"

"Locked in my drawer." He pushed the elevator button. "Any news on the cigarette butts I found by Madi's house?"

"Dead end. And they pulled Brown's body from the river. Fish got to it quickly, and we ran his name. No hits. Must have been an alias." He cleared his throat. "Good job on taking a copy of that drive." Hyatt ended the call.

Had his hard-nosed boss actually just complimented him? Tucker smiled and pocketed his phone before making his way back to Dolumhart's floor.

He pulled open the double glass doors and stopped cold.

Screams sounded from the inner offices. He rushed through the door beside the reception desk and down the corridor, pausing when he noted a huddle beside the fire-exit doorway leading to the stairwell.

And a woman's body stuck in the door.

Madi?

ELEVEN

Madison unleashed her Beretta and turned to Andy. "Stay here. Lock the door behind me. I need to check to see what's happening." They'd retrieved his laptop and hunkered down in the small office, but distant screams pulled Madison from their solace. Thoughts of something happening to Tucker plagued her mind. Was he okay? Twenty minutes had passed since he left. Too long for her liking.

She didn't wait for Andy's response and tugged open the door, then proceeded with her weapon raised. She needed to prepare for what she'd find.

A cluster of employees gathered around a doorway, and a lifeless-looking leg stuck out in the entrance. It was a woman. Relief washed over her that it wasn't Tucker, but she kept her gun positioned in fight mode.

"Stand back," Tucker yelled.

Something happened to a female employee, but who?

It didn't take her long to figure it out.

Annabelle Atkins lay sprawled out at the top of the stairway, her face bruised.

Someone had beaten her in the short time frame since they interviewed her an hour ago. Daniel Levine's face popped into Madison's mind and she tightened her grip on her Beretta. Had the vice president been watching from behind hidden cameras and heard what Annabelle confessed?

It had to be the only answer.

She approached the group and holstered her gun. "Tucker, what happened?"

Relief softened his taunt face muscles. "Madi, thank God you're okay. Andy?"

"He's fine. Is she alive?"

"Barely. Can you get rid of this crowd? I called for an ambulance and the paramedics should be here soon."

Madison nodded. "Everyone, back to your desks. We need room to investigate."

The employees dispersed, muttering among themselves. Their questions also raced through Madison's mind. Would Annabelle live? Who beat her? Why?

She knelt beside Tucker. "Do you think Mr. Levine did this?" she asked in a hushed tone.

"Nothing would surprise me with this case." He frowned. "There's more. Someone stole Leah's flash drive from the detachment."

"What? How is that possible with so many police around?"

His brow creased.

She touched his arm, the growing spark surging between them. Did he feel it too? She couldn't ignore her emerging feelings any longer. Was their hope for them? Would he forgive her for crushing his heart years ago? She snapped her hand back.

This wasn't the time to get caught up in any attractions. She needed to concentrate on the case. "You suspect someone in your detachment, don't you?"

"I do, but not sure who. It could be anyone."

Pounding footsteps approached. "You two again?" Teddy Atkins asked.

He and Charlotte rushed forward, setting their bags down.

"Bella!" Teddy yelled and fell to the floor beside his injured sister. He gathered her into his arms, rocking her. "What did he do to you this time?"

Charlotte raised a brow, turning to Tucker. "What happened, handsome?"

Madison grimaced at the woman's presence and then chastised herself. She needed to give Charlotte a break. It wasn't her fault they kept meeting in these unusual circumstances.

"We're not sure, but she's been beaten. We don't know the extent of her injuries. Her pulse is weak." Tucker moved back and allowed the paramedics room to work.

"Teddy, release her," Charlotte said. "We need to check her over. You know that."

He obeyed, his eyes moistening. The normally stoic paramedic was reduced to tears at his sister's condition.

Charlotte felt for a pulse. "Teddy, it's weak." She lowered her cheek near Annabelle's mouth, watching her chest. "Shallow breathing."

The duo inspected Annabelle's injuries on her

face and moved her sleeves up, exposing multiple nasty bruises.

Charlotte scowled. "Who did this?"

"We can't say for sure, but we will find out." Tucker's lips tightened.

Teddy's face turned beet red. "It was her boss. I know it."

"What makes you so sure?" Madison asked.

"He's done it before." His nostrils flared as a vein protruded in his neck. "I told her to stop seeing him."

"Is his wife aware of their affair?" Tucker pulled out his notebook.

"Not that I know. They made sure they weren't seen in public."

But yet the employees of Dolumhart still discovered their indiscretion. Who else knew?

They hadn't hidden it well enough.

Charlotte edged Annabelle's blouse up and exposed her stomach.

Teddy cussed.

Deep purple invaded the young woman's abdomen, indicating internal bleeding.

This was no regular beating. The intent was obvious.

Someone tried to kill her.

Just as those thoughts raced through Madison's mind, Annabelle's body seized before stilling. Completely.

* * *

Tucker held his breath as Charlotte and Teddy worked on Annabelle, but he didn't hold out any hope for the beaten young woman. Her injuries appeared too severe. *Lord, save her.* Even though she'd made mistakes in the past, it didn't mean she deserved any of this. Tucker clenched his fists. He would make Daniel Levine pay for what he'd done.

Teddy did compressions. "Bella, come back to me. You can't die."

His sister didn't respond.

Charlotte checked the EKG reading and grabbed his hand, stopping him. "Teddy, she's gone. I'm so sorry."

He continued to pound. "No! Leave me alone."

Charlotte glanced Tucker's way, her expression pleading with him to intervene.

Tucker pulled the paramedic to his feet. "Teddy, I'm sorry. There's nothing more you can do for her."

Teddy's eyes flashed venom. "He will pay for this. I'll kill him and you can't stop me." He raced down the hall toward the outer office.

Tucker and Madi followed the crazed paramedic.

"Teddy, stop!" Tucker yelled. "Don't do something you'll regret."

The man skidded to a stop in front of Daniel Levine's door. "He needs to pay."

"And he will." Tucker yanked Teddy back. "We need to do this the right way."

Madi caught up with the pair. "Teddy, listen to

Tucker. He knows how to help. Don't tarnish your sister's memory by doing something stupid." She gestured toward the closed door. "He's. Not. Worth. It." Her drawn-out words personified powerful intent.

The man crumbled to the floor and sobbed.

Madi knelt in front of him and rubbed his arms. "Shh. We'll find out who did this. I'm so sorry for your loss."

Tucker left the two together and eased open Daniel Levine's door. He needed answers.

He stepped inside the man's office.

And inhaled sharply.

The vice president was absent, his office in total disarray. Files strewn across the room. Table overturned. Chairs on their sides.

Someone had already been here, but the question remained.

Who? And what were they searching for?

Tucker retraced his steps and shut the door, returning to the foyer where Charlotte was helping Teddy into a chair. First, he needed to ask the pair about the morphine mix-up. "I need to talk to you both about something." He relayed the information about the tox-screen findings.

Charlotte fisted her hands on her hips, eyes blaring. "You think one of us tampered with medications?"

Madi joined in on the conversation and raised her hands. "We're not saying it was on purpose."

"Wasn't us, man," Teddy said. "We would never make a mistake like that. Must have happened at the hospital."

Could that be true?

"Thanks for your time, and Teddy, I'm sorry about Annabelle." Tucker guided Madi over to behind the receptionist's desk. "Levine is gone and his office ransacked."

"What do we do now?"

"I'm calling in Forensics and I'll get Hyatt to send other officers to secure the area. This is now a crime scene."

After placing a call to Hyatt, Tucker turned to Madi. "Don't touch anything."

She scowled. "I know that. I'm just checking her space to see if anything is out of the norm." She pushed a paper to the side, using a pen, but bumped Annabelle's computer.

Two monitors sprung to life. An email on each one.

Why wasn't her system password protected?

He couldn't help but read the brief email from Daniel Levine.

Meet me in our spot.

It was sent one hour earlier.

Madi squeezed Tucker's arm. "Is this proof he lured her away?"

"We can use it against him. If we can find him." Tucker scratched his head. "The warrant should arrive soon and it includes all documents on their system."

"You don't think their legal counsel will fight it?"

"They'll probably try, but Judge Saunders is relentless." Tucker glanced at the other monitor. An email in preview mode displayed. The sender's words at the top said: *You need to see this.*

The document below revealed reports from Human Resources about allegations of Daniel's abuse from other female employees. He pointed to the screen. "Are you seeing this?"

Madi fisted her hands. "Why wouldn't Dolumhart have fired him?"

Good question. One he wanted to take up with CEO, Brechin Cross.

The bigger question was…how did it relate to this case?

Why hadn't Annabelle tried to break off her relationship sooner? It may have saved her life. "Who's the email from?" Madison inched closer to the screen, but the name was hidden at the top.

"We need to wait for a warrant to see anything further."

Madison knew that, but hoped to find out who'd sent the document.

The front doors opened and the coroner entered. Charlotte led the man to Annabelle and later exited with Teddy.

"What now, Tucker?" Madison said, rubbing her shoulder. The pain from her wound intensified, but she promised herself she wouldn't take anything. She needed to be fully alert.

"How about you check on Andy? It's been a bit of time since you left the office. He's probably frantic."

Two hours after Tucker and Madison checked on Andy and reassured him that everything was okay, the forensics team left the scene. The coroner removed Annabelle's body from the office.

Tucker's fellow constables searched the premises but couldn't find Daniel Levine. It appeared he'd vanished. However, Tucker reassured her it was just a matter of time before they caught up with the man. His boss put out a BOLO on the vice president.

He heard from the fire marshal who confirmed the fire at her neighbor's house was arson. Madison's pulse climbed a notch, sending her heartbeat thrashing in her ears.

Tucker now held the warrant in his hand and served it to the next manager in charge. The man hadn't liked it and after their counsel inspected the document, they consented.

Not that they had a choice.

Tucker stood beside her at Annabelle's computer. "Okay, let's see who sent this email." He moved the curser and scrolled to the top. The name appeared.

Leah Peters.

Madison stumbled backward, but Tucker caught her. "You okay?"

His arms around her waist transported her back in time to the prom night when they shared a slow dance. His spicy cologne had enticed her and he'd leaned into her arms, whispering his announcement he'd become a Christian.

It crushed her heart because she knew then she'd end their relationship. She couldn't be with someone who trusted in the One who had betrayed her. God hadn't stopped the hurt she'd gone through. It was too much for her to handle.

Madison stepped back from his embrace and into the present. She couldn't deal with the memories right now. "Leah tried to warn Annabelle? This case just keeps getting more and more confusing."

"Agreed." He turned back to the screen, but not before she noted the disappointment on his face.

She'd upset the man who stole her heart.

Again.

She shrugged it off and concentrated on the computer. "What else can we find?"

Tucker maneuvered through Annabelle's calendar. "She had many meetings booked throughout the workday with Levine over the past several months."

"Do you think he is the key to this case?"

"He's definitely a person of interest." He clicked on her search engine and the browsing history. Page after page of the vice president's activities appeared. The dates were in the past few weeks. Had she been stalking him?

"What's the date on Leah's email to her?" Madison asked.

He switched back to the email.

Tucker whistled. "The morning of Leah's death."

A question popped in her mind. "Do you think Daniel knew Leah warned her?"

"With the concealed cameras around here? Probably."

Madison clicked on Annabelle's files. She found copies of employees' folders and stopped when Andy Richards's name popped up. "Look at this."

She double clicked on it and two files appeared. A résumé and one other. She opened the text document. It was a conversation transcript between Daniel Levine and the manager of the company Andy worked for in California. How would Annabelle get her hands on this? More important, was this how she knew to finger the software developer?

"We need to get back to Andy," Tucker said. "Maybe there's more in those files."

She nodded and they walked back to the office.

"Finally." Andy stood. "Where have you been?"

"Sorry for the long delay. Lots happening." Tucker pulled a chair beside Andy's laptop. "Can you show us the backdoor files?"

The employee sat back down and hit several keys on his laptop.

"Andy, were you aware Annabelle knew about your issue with the company in California?" Madison asked before sitting on the other side of him.

"What? How?"

"She somehow got a transcript copy of the conversation between your former boss and Daniel Levine."

Tucker grabbed Andy's shoulder. "She was the one who tipped us off about you."

Andy bolted upright, his eyes widening. "And now she's dead. I can't do this, Tucker. They'll get to me and my family next."

"We'll protect them. Don't you want to find out who's responsible for all this?" Madison asked.

"Show us the files, man." Tucker pulled out a notebook.

Andy clicked on a folder.

Multiple files appeared.

Tucker pointed to one marked *Medical Findings*. "Open that one."

Andy clicked on it.

A Word document opened with multiple columns and test subjects' names at the top. The rows contained each of their symptoms ranging from migraines, fevers, addictions, raised white blood count levels along with other milder ones.

Madison huffed out a sigh. "Wow. The company knew about all this and did nothing."

Tucker pointed to another file. "What's that one?"

Andy double clicked it.

A copy of an email from Daniel Levine to Andy demanding he doctor all findings so the authorities wouldn't find out about the issues Morvecet caused. The last line caught Madison's attention.

Do not tell Leah Peters about this. Our leader is adamant.

"We got him!" Madison stood. "He killed her. I'm sure of it."

"Andy, thank you for saving this incriminating email. We'll need to log your laptop into evidence." Tucker pulled a flash drive from his pocket. "But for now, can you copy all these files?"

His friend nodded and inserted the drive.

Seconds later, the evidence started to delete.

One-by-one.

Tucker jumped up. "What's happening?"

"I don't know!" Andy started pressing keys but nothing helped.

They were losing data.

"Quick, copy any ones you can," Madison said. She couldn't lose this lead.

Two files popped onto the flash drive before the rest disappeared from the screen and the fire alarm shrieked throughout the building.

Smoke permeated the area.

The building was on fire and Madison surmised one thing.

The team had gotten too close and someone wanted all evidence destroyed.

At all costs.

TWELVE

Tucker pulled the flash drive from the laptop and prayed his act wouldn't corrupt it. He didn't have time to worry. Their lives were on the line. Again.

"Grab your laptop, Andy." Tucker glanced at Madi's ashen face. How much more could she take on this bizarre day? They almost drowned, were shot at, witnessed a murder, and now they needed to deal with a fire? *Lord, why is this happening?* "We have to help the others and evacuate the building."

She remained in place.

He grabbed her shoulders. "Madi, did you hear me? We need to move."

Silence.

"Now!" He hated to raise his voice, but she'd gone into some sort of shock trance. He rubbed her arms. "Please snap out of it."

She blinked rapidly before exhaling. "I'm good. Sorry." She reached for the doorknob.

"Wait. It's probably hot. I'll do it." He moved her aside and gingerly touched the knob. Only warm. He opened the door and glanced in both directions.

Screams invaded the office. Employees scattered in every direction. Had this company never instructed them on an orderly evacuation procedure? He turned to Andy and Madi. "Keep low and follow me."

Tucker led them into the outer office. Smoke

greeted them. Not good. He glanced at the employees stumbling over each other. The company needed help in evacuating, but Tucker didn't want to leave Andy and Madi's side. He had to choose. "Madi, can you take Andy down the exit stairs to safety?" *Keep them safe, Lord.*

Madi's brow crinkled. "I don't want to leave you. You need help in getting the others out."

Now was not the time for her stubbornness to rear its ugly head. "You need to listen—"

His cell phone buzzed and he glanced at the screen. "Jenkins, where are you?"

"At the front of the building. You still inside?" Sirens sounded through Jenkins's phone.

Good, firefighters were here. "Yes, I'm sending Andy and Madi to you through the northeast exit. Can you meet them and take them to a safe place?"

"You got it. What about you?"

"I'm going to help the others." A commotion sounded around the corner. Employees were yelling at each other and Tucker needed to intervene. He clicked off and turned to Madi. "Take him to Jenkins."

She nodded and grabbed Andy's arm. "Let's go." They exited through the side door.

Tucker approached the group arguing and held his hands up, ignoring the smoke burning his eyes. "Listen, everyone. Stop. You need to exit using the side entrance. Do. Not. Gather your belong-

arlene L. Turner*167*

ings. They're not worth your lives." His raspy voice boomed authority, but would they listen?

The group stilled before hustling to the side door.

One woman stopped in front of him. "I haven't seen Ellen. She left earlier to go down to the coffee shop on the second level and hasn't been back." Tears filled her eyes. "Please find her. She's asthmatic."

"I'll clear the floor and head there. You go. Now."

She nodded and ran to the door.

Tucker low crouch-walked around to every office to ensure everyone was out. Satisfied, he sprinted back to the side entrance. Smoke assaulted him as he opened the door.

Not good.

He turned back to determine whether he should go out the front, but flames had erupted through the hallway, blocking his path. He had to risk the stairwell.

It was his only hope.

He pulled his jacket over his nose and stepped through the exit.

Smoke stung his eyes, but he pressed forward. No turning back. He rushed down the stairs until he reached the second floor.

"Tucker?" Madi's voice resonated up the stairway.

"Madi, where are you?"

"First floor. The woman told me you were going to the second." Pounding footsteps sounded. She appeared through the smoky wall that had formed. "I'm going with you."

"You should be with Andy."

"Jenkins is protecting him. Let's find this woman."

Tucker nodded and tested the second level's doorknob. Warm.

Did that mean the fire had started on Dolumhart's floor?

He guessed that was the case, but would wait for the fire chief's assessment. Tucker opened the door. "We're looking for a coffee shop. Apparently, the woman is asthmatic, so the smoke will compromise her breathing. Let's go."

They headed down the corridor, shouting for anyone remaining to call out.

No one answered.

Tightness formed in Tucker's chest, not only from the smoke but his rising frustration at the situation. Where was the woman? Had she already made her way from the burning building?

Madi pointed. "There's the coffee shop."

They hurried forward and opened the door.

The café was empty, but they had to clear the entire area.

Tucker headed around the counter and into a back office.

Madi followed.

They moved farther into the room.

The door slammed behind them and a scraping

sound caught their attention. Someone pushed an object in front of the door.

They were locked in.

And the room was filling with smoke. Fast.

Tucker's throat constricted, his legs weakening as terror threatened to immobilize him. He leaned against a wall and tried to calm his racing heart. A question niggled his brain.

How would they make it out alive?

Madison dropped to the floor to stay low in the room, panic clobbering her body. They were trapped. Had the woman from Dolumhart lured them here with malicious intent? Or was it a coincidence? She didn't believe in those.

Tucker fell beside her and grabbed her hands. "We need to pray."

She pulled away. "Pray? How can you say that? Why would God help us? He allowed this to happen." Just like He allowed every other tragedy in Madison's life. News of her adoption. Her parents' plane crash. Lucas's deadly heart attack. Leah's death.

And now this.

No, she would not trust in someone who placed so much pain in her path.

"Madi, listen to me. I don't understand how God works. I've been going through some hardship lately and I don't have the answers. However,

I know this. God. Is. In. Control." His stammered words were clear.

Was that really true? How could someone who worked in law enforcement trust in a higher being with all the evil and madness in the world?

She couldn't.

A crash sounded in the café, followed by a roar.

Flames erupted and danced under the door.

This was not from the fire raging on the top floors. Someone started another one outside the door. Were they trying to intensify the situation and kill them quicker?

The tiny office plunged into darkness.

Tucker pulled out his Maglite and shone the beam throughout the room. "Madi, check around for anything to block the flames and smoke."

Madison crawled over to the desk and rummaged through the drawers, feeling her way. Tucker's flashlight provided the occasional glimpse into the contents. Unfortunately, nothing to help with blocking out the ever-growing flames.

She gripped the chair and stopped. A sweater was draped over it. "Found something." She yanked it down and moved over to the door, stuffing it underneath. "It's probably not enough. Do you have—"

Her cell phone dinged, announcing a text and interrupting her question. She swiped the screen.

YOU WERE WARNED. TOO BAD YOUR LIFE HAD TO END THIS WAY.

Her power bars depleted.

She lost reception. "Is your cell phone working?"

Tucker checked his. "Nope. Not good." He shone the light toward the desk. "Try the landline."

Madison picked up the receiver. Silence. "Nope." She slammed it back into its cradle.

They were locked in and had no way to call anyone.

Perspiration beaded on her forehead. Not just from the growing heat, but from her anxieties.

Her fear of death just escalated. Tenfold.

"What are we going to do now?" Madison's shaky voice did little to disguise her angst. Great, now he'd know of her scaredy-cat state.

Tucker shone the flashlight in her direction and walked to where she stood. After putting the Maglite away, he took her hands and lowered them both to the floor. "We *are* going to pray. Don't argue with me."

She opened her mouth to protest but clamped it shut. Why bother? He'd pray anyway.

Maybe it wasn't such a bad idea after all. She bowed her head.

"Lord, we know You are in charge of all things. Even when we doubt. Madi and I reach out to You now. Please allow someone to find us here before it's too late. Show us what to do and thank you for loving us unconditionally. In Jesus' name, amen." He shifted but still held her hands. "Now we wait."

Her palms perspired, but she resisted the urge to pull away and scratch them. "There must be something we can do." She coughed from the deepening fumes blanketing the office.

He wrapped his arms around her and held her tight. His embrace helped soothe her uneasiness. Slightly. She longed to stay in this position if it meant all her troubles would disappear.

However, the roaring outside the door increased with every second, and a cliché wedged in her mind.

They were running out of time.

Suddenly, Tucker jumped up, unleashing his Maglite once again. "I want to see something."

She brushed off her fears, determination setting back in, and stood. "What are you thinking?"

"This building is older. Perhaps it has pipes that would cause a vibration if we banged on them. It's a long shot, but they might hear us. Firefighters should be dispatched throughout." He shone the light around the room.

Madison pointed. "Over there."

An old radiator sat in the room's corner.

"Perfect." He rushed over and banged the pipe with his flashlight. "Come sit. This might take some time."

Time they didn't have.

Madison walked over and slid down beside him,

waiting for someone to hear their desperate and homemade beacon.

He clutched her hand with his free one.

An ache she never realized would happen returned. Ache for the love she once had with this amazing man. Could she open her heart again? Or was it too late?

Smoke slithered under the door despite their attempt to block it. It rose higher and her throat constricted, eyes burning. Breathing became almost impossible and just as she felt herself drifting into unconsciousness, raised voices sounded from outside the closed door.

Had God heard Tucker's desperate prayer?

Tucker stumbled to his feet, bringing her with him. He banged the door. "In here!"

A scrape sounded in the café. "We're coming. Hold on!" a muffled voice said.

The door burst open and firefighters came into view. Two stepped into the room.

Madison's muscles released slightly, relief flooding her. However, they still had to get out of the building.

And how much smoke inhalation had they suffered?

Thirty minutes after the firefighters had cleared the corridor and led them to an exit on the opposite side of the building, Madison surveyed the crowd of employees gathered in the parking lot. She wanted to find the woman who had told Tucker and her about the person needing help in the second-floor coffee shop.

But she was nowhere to be found.

This confirmed they'd been set up by a different Dolumhart employee.

One who hadn't been on their radar.

Until now.

Tucker led Madi to his cruiser after being checked over by a doctor at the hospital. They both had looked for the suspicious woman, but it seemed she had disappeared along with Daniel Levine. No employees recognized Tucker's description of her or were just not talking. Plus, they didn't know of any Ellen with asthma that worked for Dolumhart. Clearly, Tucker and Madi were duped into looking for a coworker who didn't exist.

Tucker also found out from Jenkins that he moved Andy and his family to the safe house under watchful protection. Once they'd resolved the case, they'd allow them to go home, but Tucker wanted them to stay there for now. Just in case.

The fire chief confirmed the fire started on the fifth floor with the point of origin being Daniel Levine's office. Had he started it to hide Dolumhart's secrets? Or his own?

Tucker kneaded the knot in his neck. He was ready for this day to end. However, they were now on their way to Leah's home to follow up on the secretive lead on her laptop. Madi hoped to find the additional evidence Leah alluded to, but would they succeed? Plus, he wanted to look at the two files they saved to the flash drive, which was safe in his pocket. He prayed that the one locked in his work drawer hadn't been touched.

Tucker glanced over at Madi. She sat back, resting her head with her eyes shut. Her complexion told him she was weary and needed rest, but she wanted to make this one stop before heading back to her home in Saint Andrews. He admired her perseverance and the memory of their embrace earlier in the café's office sent old feelings rushing back like a dam overflowing. What he wouldn't do to keep her in his arms. Forever.

But his possible Huntington's condition erased any hope of a future with her. *Why, Lord?* Once again, he wrestled with God. The unknown paralyzed him, but he couldn't bring himself to get tested. He didn't want to know.

He pulled into Leah's driveway and studied the red brick townhouse—a three-story home with neighbors on both sides. A majestic red maple tree stood tall in the middle of the well-manicured lawn, protecting the house with ample covering.

"Are you ready for this?" Tucker asked.

Madi sat up. "I guess there's only one way to find out." She climbed from the vehicle.

He followed her up the steps. "Where's the key? Please don't tell me it's under the flowerpot."

She snickered. "This isn't TV, but you're not far

off." She counted three bricks under the mailbox and tugged on it. It released and she slid out the key. "Still there."

"Does she have an alarm system?"

"Knowing Emerson's protectiveness, probably." She inserted the key and turned. "Here we go."

He held his breath as she opened the door and waited for a piercing alarm to sound.

But none came.

Madi stepped inside and pointed to a white box on the wall. "Yup, she has one but apparently didn't set it yesterday morning. Probably too much on her mind."

He followed her into the tiny foyer. "Stay here. I'm going to clear the house first."

Ten minutes later, Tucker returned. "All clear. Okay, where do we start?"

Madi scratched her head. "What was it she said again?" She paused and tapped her finger on her chin. "Right. It's hidden in a place where she finds comfort."

"Any ideas?"

"Well, her favorite place to read was a little cubbyhole on the third floor. She said it relaxed her." She took a step on the stairs but hesitated, her shoulders slumping. "I'm not sure I can do this."

"Do you want to come back tomorrow? It's already 6:00. You're probably famished after this crazy day."

She grabbed the railing. "No, I'd rather get it over with. I *have* to do this." She continued up the steps.

He followed her to a small room at the back of the townhouse. It held a tiny fireplace, an enormous bookcase and two comfy-looking chairs. "Wow. I can see why she liked this room. It's every reader's oasis."

She turned. "Do you still read a lot?"

"Yes. My favorite is Steven James. You?"

"James Rollins. His mysteries capture me every time." She turned back to the room. "Okay, where would she find comfort? Please don't tell me she hid it among these many books."

"We could be here all night." He pulled a DiAnn Mills novel from the shelf. "Let's get started."

Two hours later after searching as many books as they could, Tucker wiped his forehead. "Okay, she probably didn't hide it in a book." He eyed the chairs. "Check under the cushions."

They tore the chairs apart but found nothing.

"Okay, maybe it's not this room." Madi slumped against a wall. "Think, Madison, think."

She popped forward and snapped her fingers. "Wait! She once told me she took solace in reading her Bible before bed. She keeps it in the family room on the second level." She ran into the hall and down the steps.

He followed her into the medium-sized room.

Madi yanked open the end table drawer beside a rocker by another fireplace and pulled out a pink Bible. She held it upside down and fanned the pages.

Nothing.

Madi plopped onto the rocker, defeat contorting her beautiful face.

"It's time to call it a day, Madi. You're tired."

"Maybe you're—"

A crash sounded below, stilling the night.

Someone was in the house.

Madison bolted from the rocker and pulled out her Beretta, alarm flooding her body as her limbs turned to jelly. How much more could she take today? *Get it together. You've trained in defensive tactics.* Did the gang follow them here or did they have Leah's home on their radar?

Tucker raised his index finger to his lips, indicating for her to be silent. He eased the door shut. He pulled out his cell phone and quietly called his unit for backup.

He didn't have to worry. Right now she was at a loss for words.

Footsteps pounded up the stairs, inching closer to their location. She glanced around. Should they hide? Where?

Tucker raised his weapon and gestured her to get behind him.

You don't have to tell me twice. After that thought raced through her mind, she silently scolded herself for her terror-stricken state. She inhaled a deep breath and gripped her gun tighter.

"We know you're here," a voice boomed. "Give up what you found and we *might* let you live."

Might? Hardly. She realized they wouldn't after all the times they'd tried. Once again, the thought of death overwhelmed her, creating panic.

"Constable Reed, we only want her."

The voice's heinous laughter pulsated shivers throughout Madison's back.

The lights snapped off.

She grabbed Tucker's arm. "Don't let them take me," she whispered.

"Never. My team should be here soon, but is there a back way out of here? Like a fire escape or something?"

She pointed to the doors. "There's a deck on this level and it leads to her backyard."

"Let me check to see if anyone is out there." He slid open the double glass doors and peered out.

The moonlight illuminated Leah's family room.

"I don't see anyone below, but they could be lurking behind those trees along her fence line. Stay here." Tucker stepped outside.

Bullets slammed into the door above Tucker's head.

He ducked and ran back inside. "Okay, now they have our location."

"What do we do?"

"We're sitting ducks here, we need—"

"You're trying my patience," the assailant said. "Give us the flash drive and we'll leave. Don't, and we start shooting."

How did they know they had a flash drive? Was this a Dolumhart employee or were there cameras in that office Andy didn't see?

Madison tugged at his sleeve. "We can't give it to him. We need it to bring these people to justice. For Leah."

He pushed a strand of hair from her face. "But I won't let them hurt you. The drive isn't worth your life."

Footsteps sounded on the hardwood floor and headed in their direction.

Tucker raised his gun and pointed it at the room's entrance, staying away from the patio doors.

Madison matched his stance.

And held her breath.

The footsteps inched closer.

Sirens pierced the night.

Thank You, God.

Even though she'd fought it all these years, her Christian upbringing raced into her head.

Would He save them? Hadn't they been through enough today?

Somewhere in the fogginess of her mind, she registered a door crashing open and pounding footfall in the house. Someone yelled, "Police! Stop!"

Glass shattered in the room next to them, followed by a thud outside. The assailants had jumped out the window to the ground.

Tucker held his gun and yanked open the door, keeping out of the line of fire. "Stay here. I'll investigate." He eased into the hallway. "Constable Reed here. Are we secure?"

Madison stood in the doorway as Tucker edged closer to the stairs.

"They've escaped," Jenkins yelled from the first level. "We're pursuing on foot. You guys okay?"

"Just a little shaken. Hard day."

"Understood. Perhaps let us handle this and get Madison home." Jenkins radioed for the officers on foot to give him an update.

"Good idea." He turned back to Madison. "Agree?"

Tucker wasn't wrong. It had been a hard day. Her body couldn't take much more. "As much as I want to find what Leah hid, I might drop soon if I don't eat and get some rest."

"Let's go." Tucker spoke to Jenkins on the way out, asking him to report any findings.

Tucker drove Madison to her vehicle and then followed her home. Said he didn't care it was out of his way. He wanted to ensure she got home safely.

An hour later after enjoying a quick bite together and Tucker reassuring her that someone will be stationed outside her home for protection, Madison said goodbye to him at the door. It had been ten years since they'd seen each other, but she felt like it was only ten days. Their friendship had rekindled quickly, even though she had broken his heart.

Was hers opening a crack to let him back in?

You can't, Madison. She sighed and closed the door. He would never take her back after the hurt she'd caused. Plus, she couldn't go through the pain of losing someone all over again. Determination stepped in and closed the crack shut. Permanently. It was for the best.

Twenty minutes after chatting with Brenda about her day, Madison crawled into bed—even though it was only nine o'clock. Squeaky jumped onto her pillow. The kitten's nightly spot. Madison chuckled and pulled her ocean-blue comforter over her, letting its warmth bring her to a state of protectedness.

She eyed Leah's box on the chair close to her and sat up. Dare she look through the contents again? Frustration had set in when they hadn't found whatever her sister hid in her comfort spot. Wherever that was. She got up and brought the box over to the bed, rummaged through it. A folded paper at the bottom caught her eye. She pulled it out.

It was a printout list of all employees at Dolumhart with four names circled in red. Daniel Levine, Andy Richards, Brechin Cross and Annabelle Atkins. Did Leah suspect these individuals? They had identified Andy's involvement and that Daniel and Annabelle were having an affair, but nothing about the CEO, Brechin Cross. They needed to dig deeper into the man's activities and background.

She grabbed her cell phone from the nightstand and hit Tucker's speed-dial number, hoping he wasn't sleeping.

He picked up on the first ring. "What's wrong, Madi?"

"Nothing. Found something I needed to share. Were you sleeping?"

"Hardly. I'm still sitting outside your house."

She straightened. "What? I thought you were getting another constable to do that?"

"I needed to do it myself. Madi, someone is trying to kill you and I'm not about to let that happen."

"You're sweet, thanks." This man's compassion overwhelmed her.

"What did you find?"

"A printout list of employees at Dolumhart. Leah had circled four names. Daniel, Andy, Annabelle and Brechin Cross. This leads me to believe that Leah suspected each of them of something."

"Do you think Cross is involved?"

"I do. Can you put his name through your database?" She eyed the envelope with her name on it in a foreign handwriting and picked it up. "Tucker, ask another constable to patrol the area. Go home and get some rest. I set my alarm and have my trusted Beretta. We're safe."

"We'll see. Have a good sleep. Chat tomorrow."

"You got it." She hung up and turned the envelope over, curiosity capturing her. A lined Post-it note from Leah was attached.

Sissy,

Mama gave me this letter to give you when the
time was right. She said it explains why she
gave you up years ago. She never told me the
reason, but said it was for my protection. Not
exactly sure what that meant, but I'm putting
it with my box of things to give you in case
something happens to me.

I love you.

2I&B,
Sissy Leah xo #SistersForever

Madison wiped a tear as she opened the envelope and removed the letter.

Dear Madison,

I want to start with three important words. I
love you. I regret giving you up, but I had no
choice. Emerson would have taken Leah away
from me. A consequence for my indiscretion.
You see, I fell in love with a ranch hand, but
for his protection, I can't tell you his name.
Emerson promised he'd ruin him if word of
our affair ever got out. My husband is a ruthless and powerful man. His political aspira-
tions drive him.

Perhaps it was my punishment. I don't
know. I wasn't a believer when it happened,

but became one later. God's love and Leah's are what I cling to now. I'm dying and I can't even hold my younger daughter. That's a regret I will take to my grave.

I gave this letter to Leah to give to you at the right time. She doesn't know any of this. She dotes on her father and I just couldn't bring myself to bad-mouth him.

I've followed you throughout your entire life, and I'm so glad you had parents who loved you very much. Their deaths deeply saddened me because I figured you'd be devastated. I wanted to tell you then, but Emerson had just won his first political race.

I'm proud of the woman you've become. I love you very much and pray I'll see you in Heaven one day.

Until then,
Your mother—Rose xo

Madison swiped at the tears flowing down her face. Her mother had loved her—from a distance. Madison wished she would have reached out, but Emerson prevented that. Why? And was her biological father alive?

Her cell phone buzzed. Who'd call her this late? She swiped the screen. Unknown caller.

She hesitated before clicking Answer. "Hello."

"Madison, it's Emerson Peters. Sorry for calling late."

What? His timing was uncanny.

"What can I do for you, Mr. Peters?" She gripped the phone tighter, her anger bubbling somewhere in the distance.

"Please call me Emerson. I was hoping you'd speak at Leah's memorial service tomorrow."

Had they released her body that fast? And why the change of heart about Madison? He knew who she was. "Sorry for being blunt, but why me? You kept me from my real mother. Why now?"

"I've lost my daughter." His voice cracked. "You're all the family I have left."

"I'm only your stepdaughter. Nothing more." The anger reached the surface and she couldn't contain it.

"I know, but you were important to Leah. Please do this for her. Not me." His voice sounded sincere.

She let out an audible sigh. "I will. For her."

"Thanks. See you at 2:00." He named the funeral home and hung up.

Madison let the phone slip from her hand, shock setting in on what just happened. Her heavy eyelids reminded her of much-needed sleep. Thoughts of Emerson Peters would have to wait until tomorrow.

Hours later, a scream woke Madison and she bolted upright. Squeaky dashed off the bed and out of the room.

Bren?

Was someone in the house? Her alarm clock read two-thirty.

She pulled her Beretta from her locked box and grabbed her phone, punching in Tucker's number. She only hoped he hadn't listened to her and was still outside.

She prayed for protection from whatever evil lurked in the shadows.

THIRTEEN

Tucker's cell buzzed, jarring him awake. He couldn't believe he dozed off in his cruiser, as he struggled with getting a good night's rest at the best of times. Horrific crime scenes plagued his dreams. He should be accustomed to what happened on the job, but compartmentalizing was not always easy.

He swiped the screen. Madi.

Tucker sat forward, adrenaline pumping through his veins. He clicked Answer. "What's wrong?"

"Please tell me you didn't listen and are still outside?" Her whispered, frantic question boomed.

"Yes. What's happening?"

"Someone's in the house. Brenda just screamed."

"A nightmare?"

"This was not a nightmare scream."

A crash sounded through the phone, confirming the danger.

Tucker opened his door and raced to the front entryway. "I'm at the door, but it's locked. I'll go around back."

"Hurry. I'm going to check it out."

"No, wait for me. I'm—"

She clicked off.

"Ugh, Madi!" He called 911, alerting the operator to the possible home invasion and requesting officers to his location. He raced around the house and unholstered his Smith & Wesson. His heart thudded as the night air cooled him. Waves crashed against the dock below Madi's home.

Tucker reached the back door and stopped.

The lock was broken and the door ajar.

Not good.

How did they evade the security alarm? Hacker? Nothing would surprise him these days. Many black-hat hackers knew how to do anything.

He approached with caution and headed in the kitchen's direction. Raised voices sounded from the hallway. He tightened his grip on his weapon and peeked around the corner.

Empty.

"Let her go!" Madi's commanding voice alerted him to their location.

"Good, got your attention," someone said. "You're coming with us, Madison Steele. He wants you."

He?

Tucker edged closer and stole a peek into the room.

Brenda was gagged and tied to her headboard.

Madi stood with her weapon pointed toward a masked man.

Tucker stifled a gasp at the scene and uttered a desperate prayer. Then rushed into the room, stepping beside Madi. "Police! Stand down!"

The masked man cussed and pointed his gun to Brenda's head. "Constable Reed, so nice of you to join us." He sneered. "You stand down or she dies. Your choice."

Brenda's muffled scream and widened eyes revealed her panicked state. Her disheveled honey-blonde hair dangled over her face as she squirmed in the bed.

"Okay, okay. Don't hurt her. Please." Madi lowered her hands and put her gun on the nearby dresser. "Take me instead."

"No! How about you let the women go?" Tucker took a step to the left, takedown scenarios running through his head. How could he contain the situation without someone getting shot? "I'll go with you."

The man pressed the gun harder to Brenda's temple. "You don't understand, Constable. He doesn't want you."

"Who is *he*?"

"You think I have a death wish? He'll kill me if I say anything."

Lord, help! Show me a way out of this.

He had to choose between the two of them. He didn't want to lose Madi, but if he chose her and not Brenda, Madi would never forgive him if something happened to her housekeeper. She was family.

"What's it gonna be, Constable? The old lady or your girlfriend?" His mocking words rumbled in the room.

Tucker surmised a sneer lurked behind the man's mask.

Madi placed her hand on his raised arm and gently pushed down. "Lower your gun, please. I can't lose her too."

She was right.

He couldn't risk Brenda's life.

He lowered his weapon.

Footsteps approached, and a crackling radio sounded down the hall. His comrades were here.

Once again, he raised his 9mm. "It's over. You're surrounded."

Officers moved in behind him.

"You'll never take me alive." The assailant pointed his gun in Madi's direction, his trigger finger squeezing tighter.

Tucker didn't hesitate and fired, hitting him in the chest.

The suspect dropped to the floor.

Tucker rushed over and kicked the man's gun aside. He hated that he had to shoot, but he couldn't risk him getting off a shot at Madi. She stood too close and he doubted the man would have missed.

He knelt beside him and removed his mask, checking for a pulse. Weak. He pressed on his wound and turned to an officer. "He's alive but losing blood fast. Call for an ambulance."

The suspect groaned and blinked his eyes open.

Tucker didn't recognize the assailant from around the area. "What's your name and who do you work for?"

He coughed. Hard. "Cicada."

"Who is that?"

"Don't. Know. Real. Name." He raised a weak finger in Madi's direction. "Closer than—"

His hand fell to the floor, lifeless eyes staring at the ceiling.

"Where are the paramedics?" Tucker once again pressed on the wound.

Madi knelt beside him and pulled his hands away. "He's gone, Tucker."

"I hated to shoot, but he was going to kill you." He stood. "You okay?"

"Yes, thanks to you."

Brenda moaned.

Madi rushed over to her and pulled the gag off before untying her. "Bren, are you okay? What happened?" She sat on the bed.

"Something woke me. I'm a light sleeper, so it doesn't take much. I got out of bed and went into the hall." She sobbed. "That's when he grabbed me."

Madi gathered the fiftysomething woman into her arms. "Shh. It's over."

Tucker turned away from the compassionate moment to let them have their time. He approached the officer. "Constable Reed. You are?"

"Constable Marshall from the Saint Andrews detachment. Good shooting," the willowy officer said. "You stationed here?"

"MCU liaison in St. Stephen."

"Right. You're working on that joint task force. How did you get here so fast?"

"Officer Steele and I are high school friends. I'm concerned for her safety, so I staked out in front of her house." Not that he really had to explain his reasoning or anything, but he prided himself on being forthcoming with his fellow officers.

"Okay, I'll call this in and get our teams here." He grabbed his radio and moved to the room's corner, speaking in hushed tones.

Tucker moved closer to Brenda's bed.

"Why didn't you see them come in?" Madi asked.

Officer Marshall clicked off his radio. "I can answer that. It appears the assailant arrived by boat and docked at your pier. Then came up your stairs from the beach and entered from behind." He turned to Tucker. "If you were out front, why didn't you hear the boat?"

Because I fell asleep. Stupid! "I'm—"

"Constable, it depends on which way the winds travel." Madi glanced at Tucker, her brow twitching slightly as if warning him to remain silent. "There are many times I don't hear the boats."

Why would she come to his rescue? She realized he'd fallen asleep.

"Makes sense," Constable Marshall said. "Okay, I'm going to consult with the team to ensure no one else is outside lurking." He walked out of the room.

"How did you guess I fell asleep?" Tucker suppressed his annoyance with himself and studied Madi.

"Your voice was groggy." She grabbed his arm.

"Tucker, it's not your fault. This gang—who- ever they are—are ruthless. You being out front wouldn't have stopped them."

"She's right," Brenda said. "You can't blame yourself."

If that was the case, why did he suddenly feel like such a failure? Tucker stuffed his closed fists into his pockets to curb his anger from erupting. Past mistakes on cases bulldozed him, returning to his memory with a vengeance. One continued to haunt him, even though it happened when he was a rookie. He'd failed to see the suspect enter a building because he turned his glance toward chil- dren playing in the park. Not for long, but enough for the assailant to take action and kill an inno- cent bystander. That case continued to give him nightmares.

"Earth to Tucker." Madi waved her hand in front of his face.

"Sorry. Just don't like making mistakes."

"You're human." Madi's lips curved into a de- lightful smile. "I've made plenty of my own."

Brenda rubbed her wrists. "What happens now?"

"We wait to ensure they secure the scene. A team will investigate."

"Can we stay here?" Madi asked.

"I'm sorry, but no. It's now a crime scene." He glanced from Madi to Brenda. "You could stay at my mother's place. She has plenty of room. Brooke lives in Alberta now."

"How is your younger sister?" Brenda asked. "Why did she move out west?"

"She used to go out there every summer to visit our aunt Cathy and work on her ranch. She fell in love with the area and stayed." Tucker's cell buzzed. "Madi, she's also a CBSA officer."

"Cool."

He glanced at his phone. A text from Hyatt. Why was he working so late?

Computer forensic examiner has confirmed Andy Richards released the worm on Dolumhart's system.

What? Why would his friend set off the virus when he knew they'd protect him and his family? A question skulked through Tucker's mind.

Had he been lying to them all this time and was part of this ring?

Madison woke to dishes clanging in a nearby kitchen. She sat up and in her foggy mind momentarily forgot Tucker had brought her, Bren, and Squeaky to his mother's place after he told them about Andy setting off the worm. They would interrogate him today. He was no longer being treated as a victim but a suspect and would be well guarded at the safe house. They allowed no electronics in his possession.

She glanced around Brooke's room. Tucker's sister had left her high school trophies for track and field behind. A picture on the dresser caught Madison's attention. Brooke stood beside a horse with a cowboy hat and boots on. She must have been sixteen. Where was this taken? Her aunt's ranch or somewhere else?

Her cell phone played the *Jaws* theme, interrupting her thoughts. Superintendent Watson. Why the early call? She grabbed her phone and glanced at the time. What? Eight in the morning. How had she slept that long? Not surprising after the day they'd had yesterday.

She clicked Answer. "Morning, Superintendent Watson."

"Call me Sam. I heard about your day yesterday and the intruder at your house. Are you okay?" His voice held concern.

Why was he suddenly being so nice to her? She sloughed the question off and got out of bed, disturbing the sleeping Squeaky. "I'm fine. Just a little tired. How did you find out?"

"Hyatt has been sending me updates. Why haven't you?"

"I'm sorry. I've been preoccupied." She grabbed a towel and washcloth. "What's up, Superintent... Sam?"

"That's better. Just wanted to tell you Wyatt's boss got back to us regarding the assailant who attacked you at their border station. His name was Doug Allen. No prior arrests or convictions. Calais police interviewed Allen's relatives and associates, but have come up empty. Dead end. Plus, the U.S. authorities confiscated all the Dolumhart meds in the truck." A pause. "They also said there were no leads on the other suspect who fled the station. He's in the wind."

Madison pulled the zipper on the duffel bag she'd quickly packed in the middle of the night, but it stuck on some fabric and wouldn't release after numerous attempts. She suppressed a frustrated scream and shoved the bag onto the floor, knocking Winston over with it. Squeaky dashed off the bed and scampered under it. "When will we get a break?"

"Soon. I just know it. I'm praying."

Him too? Since when had he become a Christian? Seemed like everyone around her was getting on the faith bandwagon. Could she?

"Anything else?" she asked, ignoring any thoughts of reconciliation with God.

"That's it. Stay safe."

"Will do." She clicked off and tossed her cell on the bed.

Frying bacon wafted into her room and sent her tummy growling. Time to clean up.

Forty-five minutes later after devouring a tasty breakfast, they'd set up shop in Tucker's mother's kitchen. He had arrived early to cook them a robust meal, as he knew they had a busy day coming up. He also told them her house was clear and they've placed a constable on her cul-de-sac, so Bren left to go home. Knowing her, she'd have the place spic and span before Madison arrived home later today.

"What time is Leah's service again?" Tucker asked.

"At 2:00. I'm sure Emerson will have the news crew there to gain sympathy from his constituents. Anything to get more votes." *Ouch.* When had she gotten so cynical? She never really liked the man and after reading her mother's letter, it added fuel to her suspicious mind.

Tucker placed his hand over hers. "Trust me. He's a nice guy."

"Well, he did sound remorseful on the phone."

"Give him a try."

"So, will Jenkins also go to the memorial? Police presence will give a sense of protection. I'm sure Emerson will need that after losing his daughter to murder."

Tucker opened his laptop and inserted the drive from yesterday's visit with Dolumhart. "Yes. I'll be there too. For you and to scope out the crowd. Sometimes suspects attend services to snoop and stay updated. It's that fear-of-missing-out thing."

"You mean FOMO. Yup, I have that too." She leaned back and folded her arms across her chest.

"Okay, let's see what we have here."

Madison braced herself for what they'd discover. "I'm still upset that we found nothing at Leah's house."

Tucker clicked on a folder. "Maybe we were looking in the wrong place. Anything else come to mind of where she finds comfort?"

She chuckled. "Well, I remember her hugging her stuffed—" She gasped and bolted off her chair.

"What is it?"

"Winston!" She ran back to Brooke's room and grabbed the teddy bear she'd brought with her last night. She hadn't wanted to leave it behind. She rushed into the kitchen, holding him up.

"You think she hid something in the bear?"

"Our mother gave her Winston when she was a little girl. She said it had always consoled her when she was upset." She sat and inspected the bear, turning it over and over. "I don't see any obvious openings."

"Feel it."

Madison squeezed the bear and stopped at one of its paws. "There's something in here. Do you have scissors?"

Tucker went to a kitchen drawer and rummaged through it. "Here you go." He handed them to her.

"Sorry, Winston. I promise I'll sew you up after." She carefully inserted a cut in his paw and reached in with her fingers, then pulled out a wadded piece of paper. "What is this?"

Madison unfolded the paper and spread it out on the table. "It's a map with an *X* marked on it."

"A treasure map?"

Madison shook her head. "She loved Indiana

Jones, so this doesn't surprise me. There's something written on the bottom." She raised the small lettering closer to her face.

"What's it say?"

"'It's. Here. You'll. Find. The. Means. To. Save. Them.'"

It's here you'll find the means to save them.

She read it back to him again. "What means and save who?" She set the page on the table.

"Where's the *X* showing at?"

Madison ran her index finger on the map. "This is a map of Saint Andrews, but it's missing the street names and areas." She examined it closer. "Wait, I can tell the *X* is showing right on top of the Celtic Cross memorial. Why would she go to all this trouble to keep something a secret?"

"She's separating the evidence to keep it from falling into the wrong hands and putting it in places only you would understand." He tapped his temple. "She realized one thing without the other was useless, so she scattered the proof. She was one smart cookie."

She slouched back in her chair, a rush of emotion slamming her. This told Madison that Leah figured her life was in danger. *Why didn't you tell me sooner, Sissy?*

She stood. "I don't understand why she didn't confide in me when she found out something was going on at Dolumhart. I would have helped." Tears cascaded down both cheeks.

Tucker stood and pulled her into his arms. "She was protecting her little sister. I admire her for that."

She sobbed and found comfort in his embrace.

He rubbed her back. "Madi, it's okay to grieve. You lost an important person in your life."

His spicy scent floated between them and she inhaled. She could get used to being in his arms.

But then the scene of what she'd done floated in her vision and knocked her backward. She teetered.

Tucker grabbed her, steadying her stance. "What's wrong?"

She wouldn't tell him what she'd done. No, he could never know the real reason she'd broken up with him after he became a Christian. It would shatter his respect for her in an instant. She cleared her throat and stepped away. "I'm good." *Just tell him.* She sat, ignoring her conscience. "Let's look on the drive to see what you salvaged from Dolumhart's files."

He frowned but sat and swiped his screen to bring it back to life. "You realize, you can talk to me about anything, right?"

"Yes." In her heart, she knew that. It was her head keeping her from divulging the truth.

He shifted the laptop to give her an angle to view the screen and double clicked a file.

Nothing appeared.

She groaned. "Did the worm destroy it?"

"Possibly. Let's hope the other one isn't the same thing." He clicked on it.

A manifest appeared, showing a dated Morvecet shipping list and the address of where it originated. Similar to Leah's copy but without the information redacted.

"Wait, that address is familiar." Tucker pulled up a map and typed in the street and number. "Yup, just as I thought. That's the warehouse district across from that park we used to go to. Remember?"

How could she have forgotten? It was where they had their first kiss.

She nodded, ignoring the rush of feelings from that special moment in time. "Do you think that's where we'll find all the equipment to produce Morvecet?"

"That's my guess." He flipped his screen back to the manifest and studied it. Seconds later, he sat straighter and pointed to the signature. "Look at who signed it. Brechin Cross."

Madison huffed and slouched in her chair. "Why does that not surprise me? No wonder Leah had circled his name. I bet she saw this document too."

Tucker checked his watch. "We need to go visit Andy, get a warrant for the warehouse and then mobilize a team to storm it. Hopefully, we'll have time to do that before Leah's memorial." He stood. "I'll get Hyatt on it."

Madison took her dishes to the sink and stared out the kitchen window, a thought mulling.

Would this be the day they caught Leah's killer?

The same day as her memorial? The irony wasn't lost on Madison.

Tucker clicked off his call with Hyatt and walked into the kitchen. Madi's blonde hair glistened in the sun streaming in from the window as she stared into his mother's yard. He could get used to sharing breakfasts with her every morning. If only—

No, he must shift his focus back to the case. Huntington's stole any hope of a relationship from him. He couldn't do that to a wife and family. Wait—

He drew in a sharp breath. No wonder his dad left. He didn't want his family to watch him suffer. His parents had seemed so happy together. It was the only answer. Thoughts turned to his mother. He fished his cell phone out to get an update on her condition and turned back into the hallway, dialing the nurses' station's number.

Ten minutes after the nurse put him in touch with the doctor, Tucker discovered his mother was stable. No change. For now. *Thank You, Lord.* He also arranged for a constable to guard her room. Just in case.

Madi and Tucker were on their way to question Andy moments later. Again. Would he tell them more lies? Tucker tightened his grip on the wheel as he pulled onto the highway that would take them to the safe house just outside of St. Stephen.

"I'm glad your mother is stabilized." Madison pulled her blind down to block the sun's rays. "Did you ever find out anything about the phone number she used to contact the supplier?"

"I was hoping to use it to set up a sting with Mom, but her condition prevented that."

"Have you tried calling it?"

He snapped his fingers. *Why hadn't I thought of that?* Another mistake. He removed his notebook from his pocket and handed it to her. "It's in there. How about you call it?"

She fingered through the pages. "Here it is." She dialed the number and placed her cell on the console. "How did their system work again?"

"She'd call the number and they would text her back with a location. I wonder if anything will happen since we're not using her phone."

The ringing stopped and disconnected. Seconds later, Madi's cell phone buzzed.

She picked it up. "Says Milltown Boulevard, put funds under the garbage bin close to the chocolate store—11 p.m."

"Wow, I can't believe that worked. That gives us the day to investigate further and go to the memorial."

Madison chuckled. "In other words, get ready for another long one."

Tucker turned into the safe house's driveway

fifteen minutes later. An unmarked cruiser was parked beside the shed. "Okay, let's see what Andy has to say for himself."

They walked up the steps to the front door and knocked.

No answer.

"That's odd," Tucker said. "Let me call the officer in charge." He dialed the number and waited.

Voice mail.

A quiver coiled his heart, putting him on immediate alert. He removed his gun and tried the doorknob. Unlocked. "Something's wrong. Stay behind me."

She unholstered her sidearm and stepped back.

He eased open the door and inched inside, weapon raised.

A child screamed. "Daddy, wake up!"

Tucker raced into the living room and found a girl hovering over Andy's limp body.

And the female officer and an older woman sprawled out on the living room floor.

A carbon monoxide detector screeched somewhere in the basement.

"Grab the girl and get outside, Madi!" Tucker rushed to Andy and felt for a pulse. Weak.

Tucker needed to save the others.

Before it was too late.

FOURTEEN

Madison sat beside the agitated girl on the back-yard picnic table and tried to determine what happened in the safe house. Seeing her father on the floor obviously traumatized the girl. She stared into the woods at the fence line. Tucker had gotten the other three individuals outside the house and called 911, requesting an ambulance and firefighters. Charlotte and a new partner were assessing the victims. The house was filled with CO, so how had the girl stayed awake? Firefighters entered the bungalow in full gear.

"Zoey, right?" Madison rubbed the child's arm.

The girl nodded in between sobs.

"They're taking care of your daddy now." She held hope that Andy would be okay since Tucker said he had a pulse. "Can you tell me what happened?"

Zoey turned her gaze to Madison. "I was asleep in my room and heard a beeping noise. I went to the living room. Daddy and Gramma were on the floor. I couldn't wake them up." Once again, she sobbed and stared into the distance.

Madison wouldn't get anything further out of her until they revived Andy.

Her earlier question on why Zoey wasn't affected surfaced. Maybe the firefighters could tell them after they assessed the situation and cleared the house.

How had this happened so quickly, and why didn't the detector alert them from the main level?

Tucker walked into the backyard with a stumbling Andy.

Madison tapped Zoey's shoulder. "Look, sweetie."

"Daddy!" She bolted off the table and straight into her father's arms.

Tucker sat beside Madison. "They're all okay. Andy's mother is being rushed to the hospital as her condition was the worst. Constable Black said she'd take Andy and Zoey in to get checked too."

"Did the constable tell you what happened?"

"She doesn't remember much, but Constable Black said Andy and his mother came into the room after breakfast. They sat on the couch talking and she felt a sting. The next she remembers was waking up outside after I hauled them from the house. Charlotte found a small dart in all of them. Seemed like the assailants tranquilized them first. Probably to subdue the group to get by them and turn on the gas. The firefighters should be able to find out more information. Our team is on their way here."

"Were you able to question Andy at all about the worm virus?"

"Swears on his mother's life it wasn't him. Nothing in his body language says he's lying." Tucker pulled out his notebook. "He said any smart hacker could have made it appear like he unleashed the worm from his IP address."

Madison exhaled. "Why am I not surprised? Probably the same woman who led us astray yesterday. Nothing in this case makes sense. How are they staying one step ahead of us every time?"

"No idea. Let's hope—"

"Constable Reed?" A muscular firefighter approached.

Tucker hopped up from the picnic table. "Yes."

"I'm Fire Chief Gallagher. Oh hey, Madison."

"Good to see you again, Chris." She stood and waved them farther into the yard. She didn't want Andy and Zoey to hear their conversation. "Can you tell us what happened?"

"Someone disabled all the main-floor CO detectors and then released the gas by covering outside vents and starting the fireplace in the living room."

"But why wasn't Zoey affected?" Madison asked.

"From what we can tell, she slept in a basement bedroom." He adjusted his helmet. "Good thing you both arrived when you did. You saved their lives. The gas would have overpowered the girl fast if you hadn't taken her outside. Paramedics will check her out too."

"Any signs of how they entered the house?" Tucker asked. "We'll do a full sweep once you give us the all clear. Just wondered if you noticed anything."

"We found the back door jimmied open."

Someone called the chief's name from the front.

"Gotta run. Your team won't be able to enter for a few hours."

"Thanks, Chief." Tucker shook his hand.

He nodded. "See you around, Madison."

She waved goodbye. "Okay, what do we do now? We have other leads to follow before Leah's service."

"Let me contact Hyatt to see if he got the warrant for the warehouse and we'll go from there."

Two hours later, Madison and Tucker sat in the park across from the warehouse. They had changed and dressed in civilian clothes to stake out the premises before the team stormed the building with their warrant.

Madison studied Tucker's profile. His chiseled chin held hints of an emerging five-o'clock shadow and she decided she preferred this look to his clean-shaven one.

Did she really just think that? It must be the memory of them sitting in the same spot when he kissed her for the first time years ago that brought it back. How could she erase that moment from her brain? She needed to in order to move on and not let her feelings grow.

Who was she kidding? They already had ever since she'd seen him the day of Leah's accident. They'd snuck up on her, taking her off guard.

How could she snuff them out?

When would she learn that love was just not in her future? She wouldn't suffer the pain of loss again.

"Do you remember this spot?" Tucker asked.

"Of course. What's-her-name had just broken up with you and crushed your heart."

"Sarah. Yes, she'd decided she liked the linebacker more than me. However, that's not what I was referring to."

Madison studied the ground, fearful of what her face would reveal. "I know. It was our first kiss." She shifted her gaze back to his baby blues.

He moved a strand of hair off her face.

She flinched from the simple touch.

"Madi, tell me the truth. Why did you break up with me?"

She jumped up. "I can't. You'll never forgive me." She stiffened her arms at her sides, trying to erase the memories of that night.

"Forgive you? I did that years ago. Nothing you say will bother me."

How could he claim that if he didn't know? There was no way they'd be friends when he learned the truth.

Besides, too much time had passed for them ever to start something new. Too much hurt. Not only from their prom night, but Lucas's death.

He tugged her arm and pulled her back onto the bench. "I can take it. I promise."

She chewed on her lip, contemplating what to say.

"Tell me, please."

Painful memories from finding out about her adoption plagued her, rushing heat to her face. Betrayal from her parents. Betrayal from God. Fine, if Tucker wanted to find out, she'd break his heart.

Again.

"You became a Christian and I became an atheist."

There. She'd said it.

Well, not all of it.

Tucker recoiled, pulling away from their nearness. Why would that make her break up with him? There must be more. She still hadn't learned to trust him.

"See, I told you it wasn't good. Now you hate me." Madi flattened her lips, a tear rolling down her cheek.

"Is that what you think? I could never hate you, Madi." It was the truth. In fact, his rebounding feelings proved one thing to him.

He still loved her.

Tucker moved closer and wiped the tear with his thumb. "Why won't you trust me with everything? There's more to your story."

She looked down.

He tipped her chin back up and stared into her ocean-blue eyes. The memory of her lips on his from their teenage years rushed him with the desire to relive that moment. He leaned in.

Her eyes widened, shock settling on her face.

It was enough to snap him back to reality.

She wasn't a Christian and he may have Huntington's.

Don't start what you can't finish, Tucker.

He scolded himself for even thinking about a relationship with her. He needed to keep himself in check.

"I'm sorry," he said. "Forgive—"

His radio crackled, interrupting his statement.

"Constable Reed," Jenkins said. "We've secured the perimeter. Only a few employees inside. No one surrounding the building. Your call. Do we move in?"

Tucker stood and pulled Madi to her feet. "We haven't noticed any movement either." Well, when he was paying attention. Would he pay for the mistake of shifting his focus to her for a few minutes? "We're getting into position. Wait for my signal."

"Copy that."

He drew his gun. "We okay?"

Madi removed her Beretta from the back of her jeans. "Let's do this." She walked toward the entrance.

She'd ignored his question.

Keep your head in the game.

He rushed forward and positioned himself in front of her. They approached the warehouse entrance. "Stand to the right of the door."

She nodded and did as he instructed.

Tucker pressed his radio button. "Teams ready?"

One by one, they acknowledged themselves.

"On my mark." He glanced at Madi. Her focus held steady on the door. "Three. Two. One. Go!"

Tucker whipped it open, raising his weapon. "Police! Stand down."

Other teams entered from different doors, shouting for surrender.

Two guards standing near the entrance pulled out guns and pointed them in their direction.

Tucker and Madi dove to take cover behind a concrete beam.

Bullets slammed into the wall close to where they'd been standing.

"You're surrounded," Tucker yelled. "Give yourself up peacefully and no one will get hurt."

Another round of gunfire greeted his command.

"He'll never let us surrender," a guard yelled.

"Who's he?" Madi asked.

"Not sure. Just that he's always watching and knows everything."

Tucker shifted his stance and peeked around the column. "We can protect you."

"You can't. Not from him." A voice came from the shadows.

"Why not?" Madi stepped out from behind her hiding place. "We can put you into witness protection if you help bring him down and testify. He killed my sister."

"Madi, what are you doing? Stay under cover." Tucker's pulse quickened.

She turned back, her eyes flashing. "I can't. I need this to be over."

Tucker bolted from his position and shielded her by stepping in front. "You have a death wish?"

She opened her mouth to speak but quickly closed it.

Now wasn't the time to argue. Tucker turned back to the group. "You, in the dark. Show yourself."

Daniel Levine stepped from his hiding place into the light.

"You. Did you start the fire and use an employee to lure us to the coffee shop?" Tucker's face flushed as anger threatened to explode.

"Of course. Tessa also unleashed the worm. You won't find her though. She's left the country. I paid her well." He sneered. "Orders from Cicada."

"Who?" Madi asked.

"Cicada never reveals his identity." His right brow twitched.

A nervous habit? Or was he lying?

Tucker had to keep him talking. "Did you kill Annabelle?"

His guards moved to surround him with protection.

"I didn't mean to." Daniel's lip quivered for a split second before composure cemented his face.

"I loved Bella, but she gave me no choice. She had to pay the price for deceiving me."

Madi stepped closer. "What about my sister?"

"She was a nuisance and was going to expose our operation. I couldn't allow that to happen, so I had thugs change her brakes." He scoffed. "You'd be surprised how fast it can be done."

Madi raised her Beretta, inching closer. "You killed Leah." She lifted the gun higher.

"Madi, no!" Tucker stepped in between them, shielding Daniel. "Tell us more. You're behind the tainted Morvecet?"

"I'm not the only one."

"Did you distribute it too?" Tucker needed to keep him talking.

"No, we left that one to someone special."

Hopefully, they'd meet that person tonight with their sting operation. He prayed that would happen. "Who?"

"Cicada wouldn't tell us."

"Who is Cicada?" Madi thrust her gun closer into Daniel's face.

"I don't know." Once again his brow twitched.

He's hiding something.

"You're lying," Tucker said. "Tell us."

Shuffling footsteps nearby told him his team was advancing. Could he keep this situation contained or would someone get hit in the takedown?

Daniel heard it too and pulled out a gun hidden behind his back.

His guards once again raised their rifles.

"He wants you dead." Daniel pointed his gun in Madi's direction. "I want you dead too."

Daniel's trigger finger twitched.

A smoke grenade clattered across the floor, creating a wall of fog.

Tucker shoved Madi to the ground, protecting her body with his as a shot fired. He waited for the sting, but none came. Multiple bullets flew.

Then silence.

He glanced up.

The obstructing smoke dissipated, rising to the high ceiling and clearing Tucker's view.

A guard lay on the floor, clutching his arm. His weapon beside him.

Daniel Levine and the other guard were nowhere to be seen.

Jenkins and his team stood with their weapons raised.

Thank You, Lord.

Tucker scrambled to his feet, searching the room for further danger. "Where did Daniel go?" He pinched the bridge of his nose, replaying the scene over and over in his head at how they could have done things differently. Had he made a mistake or had Daniel accounted for every possibility?

"Too much commotion," Jenkins said. "We couldn't see from all the smoke."

What? How did the trained officer let Daniel escape?

Tucker stood over the guard. "Who is Cicada?"

The man groaned and his fingers reached for his gun. "Why, it's—"

A shot fired, crimson moistening the man's white shirt.

Tucker turned to see who discharged their gun.

Jenkins. "He was going for his weapon. I couldn't risk him killing anyone."

"He was about to tell us Cicada's real name," Tucker said.

Jenkins had taken out their hope of identifying the ring leader.

Was it really Daniel or someone else?

Madison stood beside Emerson Peters at the gravesite as they watched Leah's coffin lowering into her resting site. Madison had spoken earlier about how she'd just found her loving sister, but they'd become close fast—to infinity and beyond. Emerson had talked about his daughter being in Heaven and that he would one day be there to meet her. Did Madison believe that? Could she put her hope in the unknown? She wanted to hold on to that promise, but her skeptical mind kept her from grasping it. Why couldn't she just let go and surrender?

Tucker's team had secured the scene at the warehouse and scoured the premises for evidence, but didn't find any. Probably Daniel and his team removed everything before the police had arrived.

Obviously, they'd known they were coming. How? Tucker stood watch from the back of the crowd who'd gathered in the graveyard, scanning for anything suspicious.

The guard had gone to his grave without revealing Cicada's identity. However, they told Emerson who killed Leah and that it wouldn't be long before they apprehended Daniel Levine. The politician was grateful, but a thought lodged in Madison's brain as she too studied the faces of those around her.

Who was Cicada and when would he strike again?

This wasn't over. They still had found nothing to help them stop the effects of Morvecet.

Hopefully, they had halted any more shipments from crossing the borders or being distributed across Canada.

Time would tell.

Emerson touched Madison's arm, thrusting her back to the moment. "Thank you for your eulogy. Leah would have been proud."

She studied her stepdad's handsome face for any signs of hostility, but there were none. Had he learned to accept her? A product of his wife's affair? "Thanks. I miss her so much." Her voice quivered and a lump clogged her throat.

He pulled her into his arms. "Me too."

She tensed at his embrace. Could she learn to trust him?

Tucker approached. "You both did awesome. That was hard."

Madison stepped back from Emerson's hug. "It was, but I'm glad I did it. It will help bring closure." Eventually. Grief took time.

Tucker's softened expression melted her previous anger toward him after their talk in the park. Perhaps he didn't hate her after her confession. Well, her half confession. She still hadn't told him about what she'd done that night with a group of kids. He'd definitely not want to be her friend or anything else if he found out. And she didn't blame him. Her stupid decisions still haunted her to this day.

"Thank you both for solving Leah's murder. I'm glad this is finally over. Well, almost." Emerson adjusted his black silk tie. "Now I can refocus on my campaign."

"I'm afraid this isn't over yet," Tucker said.

Emerson's eyes widened. "What do you mean?"

"Daniel and Cicada are still out there and until we catch them, this drug remains on the street." Tucker moved closer to Madison's side.

"Well, with you two on the case, it won't be long," Emerson said.

"Did you notice anything suspicious during the memorial or here?" Madison shifted her stance, moving her feet. High heels in the grass were never a good idea.

"Nothing," Tucker said. "You?"

"No. Emerson, did you see anyone in the crowd you didn't recognize?" Madison knew he was familiar with most people in the area because of his political status.

"I haven't met all her friends, but I did see some and a few of my campaign workers. No one stood out to me as suspicious though."

Madison glanced at the remaining people lingering. Nothing about their actions caused alarm. They simply tossed roses into Leah's grave and paid their respects before leaving.

Emerson touched her arm. "Madison, dear, I want to get acquainted with you better. I'm sorry I never tried when you and Leah first found each other. Can you forgive me?"

Once again, she studied his face. Nothing other than concern etched the lines in his forehead, but words from her mother's letter floated through her mind. Could she put the past where it belonged?

In the past.

Perhaps it was time.

"How about we start over?" After all, he was the only father figure she had right now. Perhaps Emerson knew who and where her real father was. "I'd like to get to know you better, as well."

"How about coffee at Border Junction Café tonight?"

"I'm sorry. I can't. We have a work meeting. Tomorrow night at 7:00?"

"That sounds great. I'll—" His eyes widened at something behind her.

She turned.

Daniel Levine stood with a gun pointed in her direction.

Emerson shoved her out of the way as a shot rang out.

He clutched his leg and dropped to the ground.

Emerson had saved her life, taking the bullet instead.

FIFTEEN

Tucker raised his gun, but Daniel Levine bolted into the woods. Tucker had to hustle. He called 911 asking for an ambulance and police at his location. "Madi, check Emerson and apply pressure to the wound. I'm going after Levine."

She nodded and grabbed her scarf, pressing it on Emerson's leg.

It impressed Tucker that the politician risked his life to save the stepdaughter he barely knew. Tucker hesitated.

Emerson grabbed his arm. "I'm okay. Go get my daughter's killer."

Tucker gripped his gun and headed toward the woods. He couldn't wait for other officers to get there. Levine had a head start on him.

Branches slapped him in the face as he raced through the foliage, but he kept going. He had to catch the man who just tried to kill Madi. Surprisingly, Levine had been brazen about trying to take her out in a public place, but obviously he was desperate.

That would be his undoing. Mistakes happened when someone was careless. Tucker should know.

A rustling behind a row of maple trees halted him in his tracks. He raised his gun. "Come out!"

Silence greeted him.

"You can't hide forever, Levine."

Seconds later a deer darted out and dashed deeper into the woods.

Great, he talked to animals now. He ignored the frustration setting in and picked up speed, searching for Levine.

He reached the end of the small wooded area. The VP had disappeared.

Tucker pulled out his cell and punched in Jenkins's number.

"Where are you, Reed?" the man's irritated voice boomed.

Why was he upset with Tucker? "On the other side of the woods. No sign of Levine."

"He's nowhere around the graveyard either."

"Where are you?"

"Here at the scene. Paramedics are on-site."

How had he gotten there so quickly? Had he been there the entire time? Suspicion crept in like a snake slithering after its meal. No, Jenkins must have been close by when Tucker called 911. No way was he involved.

Tucker had to trust his team. Perhaps that was why they disliked him so much. "I'm headed to you." He clicked off and rushed back through the trees and into the graveyard.

Charlotte knelt beside Emerson and tended to his wounds.

Madi leaned against an oak tree, chewing her nails.

He approached her. "You okay?"

"Irritated and thankful all rolled into one." She gestured toward Emerson. "He saved my life."

"Thankfully. He was closer than me. Who knows what would have happened otherwise." He rubbed her arm. "God intervened."

She popped up from her slouched position. "Did He?"

"When will you come back to Him?"

"When He's worthy of it." She stomped back over to Leah's grave, her high heels sinking into the ground.

Lord, soften her heart. She needs You.

And so did Tucker. His recent frustration with God held him in a vise grip. His possible disease and his mother's coma plagued him, edging him further and further from the One he once trusted unconditionally.

Why had the unknown scared him suddenly?

He set the question aside and walked to the group. "Charlotte, how is he?"

"Stubborn as usual," she said, pursing her lips.

"Easy for you to say—you're not the one in pain." Emerson's tone conveyed a mixture of frustration with a hint of teasing.

"You guys know each other?" Tucker asked.

"Doesn't everyone know everyone in St. Stephen?" Charlotte said.

"Good point." Had he forgotten how small towns work?

"I helped him with a campaign a couple years ago."

"I didn't realize you were into politics," Tucker said to Charlotte, and then turned to Jenkins. "You spot anything unusual in the past ten minutes?"

"Nothing. I'm going to consult with the other officers who are canvassing the area. I'll get back to you if there's anything of importance." He walked away.

Madi stood over her sister's grave and stared into the hole.

Charlotte and her partner moved Emerson onto a gurney and wheeled him to the back of the ambulance.

Tucker walked over to them. "Can I have a moment?"

They nodded and stepped away.

Tucker grasped Emerson's shoulder. "Thank you for saving Madi's life."

"It was nothing."

"Not true. You risked your own life to save her. I'll never forget that."

Emerson's gaze shifted to where Madi stood. "You love her, don't you?"

Was Tucker that obvious? "I can't start anything."

"Why?"

Should he tell his friend about Huntington's?

He clenched his fingers into his palms. No, he

wasn't ready to divulge his condition. "I just can't." He'd leave it at that.

"Tucker, never take love for granted." His eyes moistened. "I did and I'll never forgive myself for it."

What did that mean?

Charlotte approached. "Sorry, we need to get him to the hospital."

Tucker squeezed the man's shoulder. "Get better soon."

Madi approached the group.

"Don't you worry. I'll be fine." Emerson nodded at Madi. "I have a very important date with my stepdaughter tomorrow night that I don't intend on missing."

She smiled. "You better not. Take care."

Charlotte closed the ambulance doors. She climbed into the driver's seat and pulled away.

"When do we leave for our sting operation?" Madi asked.

"I need to check on Mom first and call Brooke. She's been texting me, asking for updates. Plus, Hyatt wants to discuss tonight's plan first." Tucker checked his watch. "I'll need some time."

"That's fine. Okay if I change at your mom's place?" She smoothed her pencil-cut skirt. "Can't go dressed like this."

"Sure. How about I pick you up there?"

"Sounds good."

At five minutes to eleven, Madi and Tucker sat in

his vehicle watching the trash can where they'd deposited an envelope of cash. Tucker had conferred with Hyatt over the plan. They'd deposit the money, wait for the distributor to pick it up and nab them.

Easy-peasy.

Right, like anything in his profession was simple.

He glanced at Madi. She'd changed into a teal-blue-plaid shirt and jeans with a brown leather jacket. She remained silent on the trip to the drop site.

"Are we okay?" he asked. He couldn't lose her friendship after reuniting with her.

She turned, her lips flattening. "We're fine, Tucker."

Were they? Her tone didn't convey that fact.

He let it go…for now. His cell phone chimed, announcing a text. His mother's doctor. Tucker read the message, his heart breaking in two. "My mother's condition has worsened. The doctor isn't holding out much hope."

Her eyes softened. "I'm so sorry." She banged the console. "There has to be something that will help."

He prayed that was true. In the meantime, he had to keep himself busy. "We need to talk about our plan for tomorrow to follow Leah's treasure map and find what evidence she left."

"I've been thinking about that." She shifted in her seat. "It has to be something significant for her to bring it all the way to Saint Andrews to hide."

"What were her words again? Something to save them."

"Right." She scratched in between the folds of her braid before pulling it out, letting her long blonde hair fall below her shoulders.

Tucker stared. He'd always loved its golden shine. He gripped the wheel tighter to resist the urge to reach over and caress her hair like in years gone by.

"What?"

Busted. "Nothing. Just thinking." Liar.

"Well, I hope whatever we find tomorrow tells us who Cicada is."

"Me too." His cell phone chimed and he fished it from his pocket. Hyatt. "An update on Emerson. They've released him."

"Already?"

"Apparently, it was just a graze, so they bandaged him up and sent him home with meds." He put his phone away. "I'm thrilled you're meeting—"

She put her hand in a stop position and pointed. "We're in business."

Tucker glanced out into the cloudy night. Storms threatened the area after a warm fall day. The streetlight shone over the trash can, revealing a hooded figure tipping it over to retrieve the envelope. Tucker opened his door. "Go time."

They approached in stealth mode and stayed close to the downtown buildings. He stepped from the shadows, right hand resting on his gun. "Police! Hold it there."

The figure straightened, dropping the package.

"Interlock your fingers on your head and turn around. Slowly." Tucker's voice commanded obedience.

Madi flanked him with her hand on her sidearm.

Neither one of them would risk the courier escaping. They could be the key in busting the distributor.

The hooded assailant turned.

It was a teenager.

"I did nothing wrong," he said.

Tucker stepped forward and patted the spindly boy down, lowering his hood. "He's not armed."

"Tell us who you are," Madi said.

"I'm just a courier for hire. That's all."

Tucker pulled out his notebook. "Tell us more."

"I watch the dark web for messages from user Shadowman and then pick up the package." The whites in his eyes shone in the streetlight's beam.

"Where do you deliver the money?" Madi asked.

"It's different every time. When I drop it off, I pick up the drugs and deliver them to the address indicated on the bottle. Tonight, I was to put it in the mailbox at Allusions Hair Creations."

Madi's jaw dropped.

Was Susan involved?

Madison held her head at the kitchen table the next morning and nursed a cup of light-roasted coffee. She needed lots of caffeine after her lack of sleep. She'd returned home defeated after the dead end with the courier. Susan was nowhere to be found; *disappeared* was the term her neighbor had used. They had questioned the courier further, but clearly he wasn't aware of anything else. Susan hadn't answered Madison's knock when they arrived at her place. Her next-door neighbor came to his front porch to have a smoke and told them he'd seen Susan stuff a suitcase in her trunk. She drove off approximately the same time as Madison and Tucker had caught the courier.

Coincidence?

Once again, she didn't believe in those. However, she refused to accept this case involved the eccentric hair stylist.

No way.

Tucker had searched for the user Shadowman, but they'd deleted the account, telling the company that they'd been watching and knew they intercepted the courier.

Plus, they still hadn't located Daniel Levine. They would question his wife later today to determine if she had information that would help their investigation and find the VP. However, Madison didn't hold out any hope.

Bren touched Madison's arm. "You okay, love? How's your shoulder?"

"Feeling better." She took a sip of coffee. "I just can't believe Susan's involved. I've known her since

I was a teenager, but the timing of her departure is just too hard not to question."

"I realize she means a lot to you, but how well do we really know what someone is going through?"

"She took Dolly's death hard, but surely that wouldn't have driven her to do something like this."

Bren walked to the stove and dished bacon and fried eggs onto a plate. "You'll figure it out. Have some breakfast." She set it in front of her.

Madison shoved it aside. "I don't have an appetite. Yesterday really took its toll on me."

Bren sat and pushed the food back to Madison. "You need to eat. Didn't you say Tucker was coming soon and you have a long day ahead of you?"

She picked up her fork. "Yes."

An hour later, she sat in Tucker's vehicle headed to the Celtic Cross at Indian Point. The place on Leah's map she had marked with an *X*.

Tucker pulled into a parking spot. "Why would Leah hide something here?"

"The monument was special to her. She told me our ancestors were Irish, and this cross is a memorial to Irish immigrants who died on Hospital Island." She wiped perspiration from her forehead. The unusually warm day promised hot temps. "Also, we spent lots of times talking here."

He squeezed her shoulder.

She flinched. Why did his touch cause her to tingle every time? Were old feelings returning?

Could she really move on from the pain of Lucas's death?

Madison grabbed the door handle. "Let's see if we can find anything."

They walked toward the cross.

Madison loved this spot and today was no different. The water stilled like a crystal mirror, reflecting its surroundings. The area was vacant since it was a weekday and fairly early in the morning.

"Thank God no one is around." Tucker stood at the water's edge. "I can understand why she liked this spot. It's peaceful."

A cardinal chirped in the distance, confirming his statement.

"It was our favorite place to come during the short—" Her voice cut out, emotion filling her throat.

He turned from gazing at the water. "I'm sorry she's gone, Madi."

Madison shoved her hands into her CBSA jacket, driving her pending tears away. "Let's search around the cross for whatever treasure she buried."

He nodded, and they both circled the cross, inspecting the memorial for hiding places.

"Well, nothing obvious," Tucker said.

"I need a closer look." She put gloves on, bent down, and ran her fingers along the cross's edge. No cracks to stuff anything into. She divided the bushes to determine if Leah dug anywhere. Madison halted when she found fresh dirt.

She almost hadn't noticed the unearthed spot, but because she was on her hands and knees, she didn't miss it. "Got something!"

"Wait." Tucker grabbed his phone. "I need to take pictures."

Madison moved aside and pointed. "There."

He knelt and inched closer.

His closeness captured her attention, feelings exploding back after years of dormancy. She ignored them and waited for him to finish.

"Done." He sat back.

She dug into the fresh dirt, holding her breath. What would she find?

Moments later, her fingers hit an object. "I feel something." She dug harder and pulled it out.

A long tin box. She brushed dirt from the top and held it up.

Tucker puffed out a whistle. "How about we take it to the bench?"

She nodded and sat beside him, setting the box in the middle. Her hands trembled at what they would find. The key to solving this ring?

She hoped.

Madison lifted the lid, the hinges creaking in annoyance.

She expelled the breath she'd been holding. The box contained three items.

A sealed envelope with Madison's name on it.

A vial of liquid and a piece of paper wrapped in an elastic.

And a tiny jewelry box.

Madison glanced at Tucker.

The bridge of his nose held wrinkled lines.

It also piqued his curiosity.

"I need to take pictures first." He snapped several. "Okay, open the envelope."

She slid her gloved fingers under the seal and pulled out a single folded piece of paper.

Madison held the note between them. It was an email containing gibberish. "Why would Leah hide this? I don't understand the words."

"Let me see."

She passed it over.

He took a picture. "Appears to be an encoded email."

"How would she get ahold of something like that?"

"No idea." His eyes widened. "Wait, let me check with Andy." He stood and walked closer to the water.

Madison opened the tiny box. Tears formed at the object before her.

Her sister's rose-gold cross pendant sparkled with a note attached.

For my sweet sister. 2I&B xo.

Madison's lips quivered. *Why, God? Why did You take her from me?*

Tucker returned and stopped in front of her. "What's wrong?"

She ignored the tears spilling down her cheeks.

She didn't care if he saw them. She held the box up. "Leah left me her cross."

"She wanted you to have a symbol of her stead-fast faith."

Was that true? Was this Leah's way of reaching beyond the grave, witnessing to Madison? Her sister knew of her struggle with past pain and had always encouraged her to seek counseling. Her words returned to Madison. *Sissy, run to God. He's waiting.*

Was He?

Would He forgive her for all her hate and defaming of His name?

She slammed the box shut. "What did Andy say?" She needed to change the subject.

"I was right. He found the email among hidden files and wanted Leah to have it. He didn't understand the gibberish." He sat back on the bench. "I sent the picture I took to my contact at the CSE."

The Communications Security Establishment handled cryptography and protected Canadian documents. Madison had studied the Government of Canada's department for a paper in college.

Tucker pointed to the box. "What's wrapped around that vial?"

She removed the elastic and unfolded the paper. And froze.

"It's an antidote with a list of combined medications to counteract the effects from Morvecet."

Madison snapped her gaze to Tucker. "That's what she meant by the means to save them."

One question remained.

Was it too late for Tucker's mother?

Tucker bolted off the bench. "We need to get this to St. Stephen. Stat."

She nodded and gathered all the items. "Let's go."

On their drive to the hospital, Madi glanced at the paper. "It says here that it hasn't been tested yet. Do you really want your mother to be the test subject? Plus, would your mother's doctor give it to her without verification?"

Tucker pointed to the vial. "I don't have a choice. The doctor said she's failing rapidly. This could be our only hope."

"Why do you think she hid this?" Madi asked. "Why not send it to the authorities? It could have helped people."

"She was probably scared it would get in the wrong hands and be destroyed since she knew they were onto her."

Two hours later after begging the doctor to at least try administering the drug, Tucker watched him insert a dosage into his mother's IV line. He'd had the lab analyze the contents before taking any risks. It satisfied the scientists that the meds included in the vial matched the list on the paper they'd given them.

The doctor turned. "This is unorthodox and I don't like it. However, your friend Emerson Peters called while I was inspecting the list of ingredients and demanded I give it to your mother. Said he'd pull hospital funding if I didn't. I couldn't risk that and the drugs used were solid."

Good. The call he'd made earlier to Emerson worked. Sometimes having a politician as a friend paid off. "How long do you think before we see any results?"

"*If* we see any, you mean. No idea." He shoved his hands into his white lab coat. "I suggest you pray and pray hard." He left the room.

Tucker sat in the chair beside his mother's bed and took her icy hand in his, bowing his head. "Lord, only You know if this will work. Please, I beg you. Heal her." He paused. "I'll never doubt you again. Give her back to me. Amen."

"Amen." Madi stepped behind him and put her hand on his shoulder. "I didn't realize you had doubts."

"I bet most Christians do at times. We're human and sometimes it's hard to put our complete trust in Someone we can't see."

A shadow crossed Madi's pretty face. What was she holding on to? He grabbed her hand. "Trust Him with whatever you're going through. He will help."

She exhaled. "The antidote is gonna work. I just feel it."

"It has to. Brooke and I can't lose another parent."

"Have you called your sister?"

"Yes, she's on her way from Alberta." Tucker glanced at his watch. "Let's grab a bite to eat and then head over to Mrs. Levine's."

"Are you sure you don't want to stay here? I can interview Daniel's wife."

He stood. "With him still out there somewhere? No way. You need protection."

Her eyes narrowed. "I'm a big girl, you know. I can take care of myself."

"Not saying you can't. Mom would want me to see this through." He grabbed his jacket. "Let's go."

Tucker sat beside Madi on Daniel Levine's leather sofa, waiting for Mrs. Levine to return with their coffees. She had welcomed them into her home after Madi and Tucker had a quick lunch at the café, but promptly rushed to the kitchen.

What's taking her so long?

Dishes clanged in the distance, so they knew she hadn't tried to run.

Madi raised her brows. "What is she doing?"

"Who knows?" He tapped his finger on his knee, his impatience settling in.

"Here we go," the fiftysomething bleached blonde said. She set a tray of sweets and their coffee on the table. "I couldn't have you here and not show you some southern hospitality. Now, help yourselves, y'all."

"Where are you from, Mrs. Levine?" Madi asked. She grabbed a plate and set a cookie on top, fingering the treat.

"Darlin', call me Goldie. I'm from Texas." She grabbed an emery board and filed her hot pink nails. "Now, what can I do for you?"

"We're looking for your husband." Tucker didn't have time to waste on pleasantries.

She stopped filing. "Daniel left on a business trip two days ago."

Tucker glanced at Madi.

She tilted her head.

It was obvious Daniel Levine was hiding from all of them, including his wife.

Tucker leaned forward. "Mrs.—Goldie, I hate to tell you this, but we saw him yesterday afternoon at Leah Peters's memorial service. Why didn't he tell you he was back from his business trip?"

She bolted out of her chair and threw the file. "He's done it again, hasn't he?"

Madi set the plate on the coffee table, the cookie untouched. "Done what?"

"He's cheating on me." She plunked herself back into her chair. "He promised. Who is it this time?"

So, she wasn't aware of the affair.

And they had to break it to her.

Tucker sighed through his teeth. "I'm afraid so. With his receptionist."

"Bella? Why I ought to give her a piece of my mind."

Madi uncrossed her legs and leaned forward. "You can't. She's dead. Murdered."

Her hazel eyes narrowed. "Good. Never did like her." She picked up her nail file and waved it at them. "And no, I didn't do it. I couldn't hurt a fly."

"Did your husband ever beat you, Goldie?" Tucker asked.

Her hand flew to her cheek and her gaze darted out the window.

Was her heavy makeup hiding bruises similar to those left on Annabelle's body?

Heat flushed Tucker's face at the thought of this man getting away with abuse all these years. "Why didn't you press charges?"

She turned, lips quivering. "You don't under-stand."

Madi leaned forward. "Help us to, Goldie."

"I tried, but Daniel has friends on the force. As soon as I tried to report his abuse, they called him to come bring me home."

Tucker tightened his muscles. "What? Who?"

"Not sure if he still does. I let it drop after the last blow. I was scared he'd kill me next time, so I accepted the fact that even the police wouldn't help me."

Daniel Levine was well connected. No wonder he'd gotten away with it for so long.

Tucker needed to bring the interview back to the pharmaceutical company. His abusive nature may be fueled by his greed to get to the top. "Goldie, can you tell us anything about your husband's job at Dolumhart?"

"Just that he's a vice president and has recently come into money." She snickered, her mood changing on a dime. "He knows how much I love his gifts. Bought me an expensive sports car and himself a fancy motor home. Said he wanted to take fishing trips."

Madi huffed and slumped into her chair.

Tucker made a note to check the motor-vehicle registration records. "Did he say how he paid for them?"

"Nope. Don't know. Don't care."

Had years of abuse walled her heart off completely?

Clearly, they would get nothing further from Goldie Levine. He stood and removed a business card. "If you hear from him or think of anything else, call me."

They said their goodbyes and walked out the front door.

"Well, that was a useless conversation." Tucker fished his key fob out of his pocket.

"Do you think she's really that ignorant of her husband's business?" Madi asked.

"Perhaps she doesn't care as she's used to a certain lifestyle."

They stepped off the Levines' front porch and down the lane to his vehicle parked along the street.

Tucker dangled the key fob. "Do you mind driving? I want to contact Jenkins and Hyatt."

"Sure." She took the keys and walked to the driver's side.

Tires screeched around the corner and a vehicle appeared out of nowhere, careening in Madi's direction.

Tucker's heart ricocheted to his throat.

He needed to save the woman he loved.

SIXTEEN

"Watch out!"

Madison's pulse exploded, a scream rising in her throat. Tucker's warning rang in her ear and the vehicle was seconds away from hitting her. She was going to die. Her fears rose to the surface, and she froze in place. Her limbs wouldn't move even though her mind willed them to run.

Strong arms circled around her waist and thrust her toward the Levines' front lawn.

Just in time.

The truck screeched down the street and disappeared around the corner.

Madison fought for air, panic encircling her body in a cocoon. Her hands flew to her throat as if that would help release breaths.

Tucker pulled her into a seated position on the grass. He called 911 and explained the situation, requesting constables to pursue the vehicle. He clicked off and turned back to Madison. "Inhale, Madi. You can do it."

How could he be so calm?

Right, he had God on his side.

She didn't.

"Do it with me. Breathe in." He took a breath and exhaled. "And out."

She copied his actions and slowly her ragged breathing steadied.

He rubbed her back. "Told you."

"Did you recognize the vehicle?"

"It was a red 4x4 pickup, but that's all I caught. I only thought about reaching you. Why didn't you run?"

"I froze." She glanced at his handsome face. Could she tell him her fears or would he laugh at her?

He caressed her cheek, brushing the escaped strand of hair from her eye. "Something made you panic other than the racing truck, didn't it? You can tell me. I won't judge."

She prayed that would be true. *Tell him.* She took in a big breath to give herself courage. "I've always been afraid of death ever since I was a little girl." She paused and wiped her sweaty palms, reliving the moment that had started her obsession with death. "When I was ten, I went against my mother's wishes and test rode a friend's ten-speed bike. I'd only ever driven a five-speed, and I wanted to try hers."

"What happened?"

"I rode it to the end of the street and turned onto the main road, forgetting it had a hill. Next thing I knew, I was flying down it and the brakes wouldn't work for me." She clamped her eyes shut as the memory floated. "I crossed the busy intersection instead of turning left. Thankfully, no cars were coming."

His eyes widened. "God stopped the traffic for you that day. That's the only answer."

Was that true?

"I don't know, but ever since that moment, death has held me in its grip."

Tucker hugged her. "When will you give your fears to God?"

Madison jumped up, away from his embrace. "Please don't preach to me, Tucker."

She brushed grass off her pants, the intimate moment disappearing in a flash.

Tucker stood. "I'm sorry. I'm just concerned."

"I'll be fine." She grabbed her cell phone. "I need to check in with my superintendent. I don't want him getting angry with me."

Her phone jingled before she was able to dial. Susan. "Susan, where are you?"

"Hey, sweet pea. My neighbor texted me saying you were looking for me. Is everything okay?"

She couldn't tell her about the drop at her hair salon. "We had further questions for you. Where are you?"

"I took Dolly's death hard, so I needed to get away. An opportunity arose and I had to leave quickly."

Tucker put his hands on his hips, his curiosity showing on his face.

She ignored him. "Okay, thanks for calling. I wanted to be sure you were safe. Take care."

"You too, sweet pea." Susan clicked off.

She turned to Tucker. "She's okay. She needed to take a trip."

"Good. You call Sam. I'm going to touch base with Jenkins to find out if he has any further information on the case." He hopped in the unmarked cruiser.

Madison punched in Sam's number and waited.

"Afternoon, Madison," Sam said. "What's happening?"

"I wanted to call and give you an update." She spent the next ten minutes telling him what they discovered within the past twenty-four hours.

A whistle sailed through the phone. "Interesting. Has Tucker heard anything back from the CSE yet?"

"No, it's too soon." She rubbed her knotted neck muscles. Should she tell him about the truck incident? He'd probably find out about it through Hyatt anyway. "One more thing. A pickup tried to run us down while at the Levine home." She said *us* since they really didn't know who the target was. No need to cause him to worry.

"What? Are you okay?"

"Fine. We were able to jump out of the way." Sort of.

Sam cleared his throat. "I need to talk to you. In person."

"About?"

A pause. Was he stalling?

"Rather not say over the phone. When can you get here?"

Odd. What was so important he wouldn't tell her over the phone? "Let me check with Tucker on what's next in our investigation. I'll get there as soon as I can."

"See you then. Be safe, Madison." His tone screamed concern.

Had his opinion of her changed? Why?

She shrugged off her curiosity and pocketed her phone before climbing into the cruiser.

Tucker clicked off his call. "Everything okay?"

"Sam wants to meet me in person about something. No idea what."

"When?"

"Whenever I can get there. What's the latest update?"

"Hyatt said that Jenkins has been following up on a lead all morning and he hasn't heard from him, which is odd for the constable."

"Do you think he's okay?"

Tucker put his cell phone back in his pocket. "I hope so. Levine is still MIA. Hyatt has put a BOLO out on him."

"Any word on the motor home?"

"Yes, we now have the make and license plate number. We have put officers on alert to watch for it. They're also searching for that red 4x4 pickup." He paused. "Oh, we should find out information from Rob, the cryptanalyst from CSE, on that note we sent to him sometime today. He said he'd make it his priority."

"Okay, so we don't have any other interviews this afternoon?"

"No, we're in a wait-and-see mode, so we can call it a day. How about I take you back to your car and you can go meet with Sam? I need to pick up Brooke anyway, and we're going to check on Mom together."

"Keep me updated on her condition. I also have my coffee date with Emerson tonight." She touched his arm. "Thank you for encouraging me to talk to him."

"You're welcome." He placed his hand on top of hers and squeezed. "Anything for you, Madi."

She let out a soft gasp as their electricity surged, and she didn't want to let go.

Their gazes locked and she eyed his lips, yearning for them on hers again. Had she worked through the pain from losing Lucas and was ready to open her heart again? And would he allow her back in after breaking his?

He moved his hand to her face, rubbing his thumb on her cheek.

Was he feeling their reconnection too?

"Madi," he whispered and moved closer.

In that moment, she wanted nothing more than for him to kiss her. She closed her eyes in anticipation.

Tucker cleared his throat.

She opened her eyes and dropped her gaze, disappointment setting in.

He didn't feel the same way.

"I can't, Madi." He started the ignition and pulled away from the curb, heading toward Madison's sedan.

Leaving behind another broken piece of her heart.

Tucker sat with his sister beside their mother's hospital bed, the scene with Madi earlier in the car rolling through his head. Why had he gotten so close again? He longed to kiss her and almost had, but he just couldn't start something. For her sake. He wouldn't break her heart like his father broke his family's.

Brooke snapped her fingers. "Where did you go, Tucker?"

His face flushed. "Sorry. What did you say?"

"Just asking about Madison. How is she?"

He glanced out the window. "Fine."

"Aww…that's what's gotten you riled up. You still care for her, don't you?"

He jerked his gaze back to his sister. "Why would you say that?"

"Because you have the same look you had after she broke your heart in high school." Brooke took their mother's hand.

"You remember that?"

"Hard to forget. You moped for weeks, Tucker. Tell me what's going on."

"You're right—I do still care for her." Not only cared for her, but loved her. Being so close with her the past few days solidified that fact. "I can't start anything, Brooke."

"Why not?"

"Because of Dad."

"You think because he had Huntington's, you do too?"

"Yes, and I can't put Madi through the pain Dad put Mom through by leaving." He stood. "Although, I understand now why he left. He didn't want the people he loved to watch him deteriorate."

"You men and your dignity!" She stood and bobbled her finger at him. "I've been tested. Have you?"

"No."

She huffed out a breath and sat back down. "Well then, how do you know for sure?"

"I don't want to."

"Big brother, don't go through life with regrets." She bit her lip. "Believe me—I know better."

"What does that mean?"

Brooke fingered the cowboy boot pendant around her neck. "Nothing. Take it from me—tell her. Before it's too late."

Tucker studied Brooke's face. What memories and mistakes haunted his little sister?

"Son, don't let love pass you by." His mother's weakened voice stilled the room.

Tucker rushed back to her bedside. "Mom! You're awake."

"Yes. Dry throat."

Brooke stood. "I'll go get the nurse and ice chips." She rushed out of the room.

"How are you feeling?" Tucker asked.

"Weak. What happened to me?"

"You went into a coma. Madi and I found what we're hoping is an antidote. We had the doctor try it on you." He rubbed her chilled arm. "Looks like it's working."

"Son, please tell me you'll give Madison a break. It's obvious you care for her."

"But Mom, I can't put her through what Dad did you."

"You need to at least tell her how you feel and give her the choice. Your father robbed me of that."

Tucker sucked in a breath, realization setting in. Was his mother right? Should he at least tell Madi?

He slouched back in his chair. No, he couldn't face her breaking his heart.

All over again.

Her rejection would rip him to shreds, and there would be no coming back this time.

Madison walked through the entrance of St. Stephens' CBSA station, trying to erase the scene with Tucker from her mind. *Stupid, Madison.* There's no way he'd forgiven her for breaking his heart all those years ago. Even if she hadn't told him the entire reason.

Once again, her heart was crushed and pain shot through her muscles, making her limbs go to jelly.

Strength, Madison, strength.

She inhaled and knocked on Superintendent Sam Watson's door.

"Come in," the muffled voice said.

She walked in and sat in the seat across from his desk, pushing thoughts of Tucker aside. "You wanted to see me?"

"Yes." He fiddled with the pens on his desk.

Something had him on edge.

She leaned forward. "Just tell me. What did I do wrong?"

"What? Nothing." He stood and walked over to her, pulling up a chair.

"What's going on, Sam?"

He took her hands in his. "I figured out something very important this week. Something I never realized until you ran out that day after your sister."

"What's that?" She pulled her hands away. "You're scaring me."

"I'm your father."

Madison bolted out of her chair. "What? How do you know that?" She walked to the window. She needed personal space.

"As soon as you told me Leah Peters was your half sister, it dawned on me."

Suddenly, words from her mother's letter flashed

in her mind. She spun back around. "Wait. You're the ranch hand who fell in love with my mother?"

He nodded. "Rose was the love of my life. We both recognized the affair was wrong, but we couldn't help it. Emerson treated her like dirt. Just a trophy wife for his campaigns." Fire flashed in his eyes, pain still etched in his forehead's wrinkles.

She stepped closer to him. Superintendent Sam Watson was her father? How was that possible? Could she deal with this right now with everything else happening in her life? "You didn't know about me all these years?"

"No. I discovered Rose was pregnant. We met in secret the night Emerson ordered her to go away to give birth. She told me all about it."

"Why didn't you go with her?"

"She wouldn't let me. Said she'd never get away from him. He wouldn't allow it." He raked his fingers through his salt-and-pepper hair. "I did what I had to do. I set her free."

"She came back though. Why didn't you ask her about me?"

He sat down and pulled her with him. "I needed to get out of town. Seeing them together brought too much pain, so I moved away for a period of time."

"Why did you return to St. Stephen?"

"I had started with the CBSA in British Columbia and did well with them. The superintendent's position opened up here and I couldn't pass it up."

"Had Rose ever tried to contact you?"

"Yes, she sent me a letter and told me you had died in childbirth. That's why I never looked for you."

Realization kicked Madison in the belly. "She was protecting you and when I told you about Leah, you realized the truth. I was alive."

"Yes."

"Why didn't you tell me right away?"

"Because of him."

She sat back in the chair, distancing herself once again. "Emerson?"

"Yes. I didn't trust him and thought he might try to spin the story somehow."

"He's changed. He saved my life yesterday."

"That's why I'm telling you this now."

She tugged at her braid. "What do you mean?"

"He called me and told me to tell you the truth. That he was a changed man. He'd come back to God." He paused. "I was skeptical at first, but the tone in his voice told me he was sincere."

Madison stared at her boss. Her father.

What were the odds?

Once again, Sam grabbed her hands. "Do you believe me?"

She nodded.

His cell phone chimed. He pulled it out, glanced at the screen and bolted out of his chair. "You need to get out of here. Now."

"What? Why?"

"I've been doing some of my own investigating and it's led me to another suspect."

She stood. "Who?"

"Constable Jenkins, and he just walked through the door with Daniel Levine."

Madison had to call Tucker.

"Can you come to the border patrol station right away?"

Tucker straightened at Madi's frantic voice. He jumped out of his chair, knocking it over. The crash resonated in his mother's private hospital room. "What's wrong, Madi?"

"Sam told me he suspects Jenkins, and he and Daniel just walked through the doors. I need you here before—"

The call dropped.

Tucker grabbed his coat. "Madi is in danger. I need to go." He kissed his mother's forehead and rushed from the room.

Five minutes later, he pulled into the border-patrol station with his sirens blaring. He jumped out and removed his weapon from its holster. He needed to protect Madi. He edged his way to the front door, staying close to the building, and peeked through the glass.

Daniel Levine had his gun thrust into Madi's temple. Sam stood to the right of them, hands raised.

Jenkins was behind him with his weapon holstered.

Why wasn't he subduing Levine? Was he really in on this?

Tucker tightened his grip on his weapon, his anger threatening to burst. *Keep it in check. You don't know the entire story.*

He needed to intervene.

Tucker burst through the door with his gun raised. "Stand down!"

Levine and Jenkins spun around.

Jenkins raised his hands, inching closer to Tucker. "It's not what you think," he whispered.

"Then tell me what *it* is."

"I can't. Not yet." He turned back to Levine. "Daniel, it's not worth it. We need to leave. Now."

The man's wild eyes darted from person to person. "How are you going to get past Constable Reed?"

Jenkins unleashed his weapon and pointed it at Tucker, tilting his head. "Don't do anything stupid. I need you to stand down."

"Not happening, man." No way would Tucker let Levine hurt Madi.

As if on cue, Levine grabbed Madi's arm and pushed her toward the door. "We're leaving. You try anything and she dies. Do. You. Understand?"

Sam stepped forward.

Jenkins pointed his weapon at the superintendent. "Don't."

He stopped, fear etched on his knotted face.

"Daniel, you should never have come here," Jenkins said.

The vice president pushed Madi closer to a side door. "She has to pay for interfering just like her sister. My life is ruined."

"Do you really want another murder on your record?" Jenkins asked.

Tucker crept closer, trying to understand Jenkins's angle. How was he involved?

Suddenly, Levine pushed Madi hard and she fell to her knees. He rushed through the door.

Jenkins turned to Tucker. "I'll follow him. You check on her. I'll explain later." He ran out of the building.

Tucker called 911, requesting back-up. He then rushed over to Madi just as Sam fell on the floor beside her.

"Honey, are you okay?" Sam asked.

Honey?

Madi nodded, rubbing her knees. "I'm fine." She glanced at Tucker. "Thank you for coming. You saved me. Again."

"What's going on, Madi?"

"Tucker, Sam is my biological father."

"What?" How could that be?

Over the next fifteen minutes, Madi told Sam's story and then explained how Daniel Levine burst through the doors, threatening to kill her. He blamed her for Annabelle trying to end things with him and her death. He had loved her and was about to leave his wife. His crushed heart couldn't take not only her breakup but her death. It put him over the edge. She had no idea how Jenkins was involved.

Sam received a call, taking him back to work.

"When I asked Daniel again if he was the ringleader, he just smirked," Madi said.

"So, we're still no further ahead." Tucker scribbled a note, frustration creeping back in. "I need to get in touch with Jenkins. See what he knows."

"How's your mom?" Madi asked.

"She's come out of the coma."

"So, the antidote worked." She pulled him into a hug. "I'm so happy for you."

His muscles tautened and she released her arms, confusion etched on her face.

"She's still weak." He'd ignore the questions he saw on her face. Questions he wasn't ready to answer. "When do you meet Emerson?"

She glanced at her watch, her eyes widening. "I need to go. I can't show up there dressed like this."

He smiled. And why not? She was beautiful no matter what she wore.

Sirens sounded. His fellow constables had arrived.

"Tell me how it goes." He stuffed his notebook away. "I'm going to confer with the constables outside and then head to the detachment to search through all the files we've accumulated. Maybe we missed something. Plus, Rob should get back to us soon."

"Keep me updated."

He nodded and left the building.

After explaining the situation to the constables, Tucker sent them in search of Levine. He jumped into his cruiser, determination crawling throughout his body. He was on a mission and would start with Jenkins.

"What do you mean, you don't know?" Tucker resisted the urge to slam his hand on his desk twenty minutes later after finally getting in touch with Jenkins. The constable had confessed he'd been following Levine for quite some time, but didn't know where he was at the moment. The vice president had evaded capture. "You need to tell me what's going on. Immediately."

Hyatt popped his head through his office door. "Reed, get in here!"

Oops. Tucker hadn't meant to raise his voice.

"Jenkins, I gotta run, but you need to tell me later why you were helping Levine." He punched off the call and shuffled to Hyatt's office.

"Sit. Down." Hyatt leaned back, crossing his arms.

Tucker was in trouble. "Sorry, Corporal. I didn't mean to get so angry. Won't happen again."

"I need to explain what Jenkins has been doing for me."

Tucker sat. "Okay."

"Jenkins has been following up on another lead and to obtain more information, I had him get closer to Levine. Pretend he was a dirty cop."

"What? Why?" More important, why keep it from Tucker? Hadn't Hyatt put him in charge of the investigation?

Hyatt pulled out a file and handed it to Tucker. "I get what you're thinking. I checked your past files. You'd made too many mistakes and we didn't trust you with this."

Tucker clenched his jaw. What would it take to earn their respect? "Those mistakes? I was a rookie, Corporal. I think I've redeemed myself."

"You're right and I'm sorry. But you're too close to this case. I know your history with Madison. We had to leave you out of it." He pointed to the folder. "Read it."

Tucker opened the file. Personal financial records, surveillance, arrest records for another Dolumhart employee. Brechin Cross. "How did you get all this information? Did you have probable cause for a warrant?"

"Of course."

"I was just about to look closer into the CEO." He glanced at Hyatt. "I still don't understand what tipped you off and made you put Jenkins on involving Levine."

His leader templed his fingers. "Check out the birth records in the file."

Tucker flipped through the pages, and his jaw

dropped. Brechin Cross was an alias. His real name was Brechin Levine. "They're brothers?"

Hyatt nodded. "We figured we could get in on the business if Jenkins turned dirty." He used air quotes around the word *dirty*.

"What did you find?"

"That the brothers hated one another. Rivalry of some sort. Flip to the Saint John newspaper article."

Tucker obeyed and read.

"Brechin Cross, CEO of Dolumhart Pharmaceuticals, was found dead at the bottom of a ravine late yesterday morning after reports of a crash. Police are still investigating the single-car accident—"

The story was dated three days ago. "Wait." Tucker stood, closed the file and tossed it on Hyatt's desk. "You think Levine killed his own brother?"

"We do but can't prove it. Yet. We think Levine was trying to silence his brother from going forward with Leah's findings and take over Dolumhart." He walked around his desk and squeezed Tucker's shoulder. "I'm sorry I didn't trust you enough with this. It won't happen again."

"One more question," Tucker said. "Mrs. Levine told us she tried to report his abuse, but someone at the station ignored her and called Daniel. Do you know who that was?"

Hyatt's jaw tensed. "That officer is in jail. Incarcerated after the drug bust Madison helped solve. Can't believe we had a dirty cop on our force." He turned to his computer. "That all?"

Tucker nodded and walked back to his desk, thankful to understand the reason Jenkins had deceived the task force and also that there were no longer corrupt cops on the team. He hoped.

Tucker inserted the drive containing Leah's copied files and once again perused through each of them, hoping he'd find something they had originally missed. He scanned the list of folders, reading the names—

And stopped.

An untitled folder appeared at the bottom of the list. How had they missed that? Was it just an empty folder? He double clicked.

A single Notepad file popped up. Tucker opened it.

A copy of an email from Brechin Cross to Daniel Levine.

Brother, here are the actual results of the Morvecet clinical trials. You lied and for that you're going to jail.

Below it was a pasted spreadsheet containing all lab results.

Relief washed over Tucker and his shoulders relaxed. They had him. Proof of a tainted conspiracy.

If only they could find Levine and put him behind bars, proving that he was Cicada.

Before it was too late and they lost other lives.

SEVENTEEN

Madison walked into the Border Junction Café shortly after seven o'clock and immediately breathed in the scent of roasting coffee beans. No wonder she favored this spot in town over others. Sam's news warmed her heart in a short time. Perhaps things were looking up for her. Even though Tucker didn't want to have anything to do with rekindling a relationship, she at least had her dad.

Dad.

She smiled at the idea of getting to know Sam better. He was a ray of sunshine on her otherwise dreary day.

Emerson waved from a table near the back of the café.

Charlotte sat across from him.

Madison tensed, irritation setting in at the sight of her nemesis. She needed to let it go and learn to accept the fact that the paramedic lived in the same area. Maybe Madison would try to get reacquainted with the woman.

Give me strength.

Charlotte slammed the table and stood. "You better." She stomped in Madison's direction. "He's all yours." The door bells jingled upon her exit.

Madison moved to Emerson and sat, placing her cell phone on the table. "What's up with her?"

"Nothing. She saw me sitting here and asked

if she could get in on my campaign, but I told her I was already fully staffed. Guess she's thinking about getting into politics." He pushed a coffee in her direction. "I ordered you a pumpkin-spice latte."

She smiled, a thought racing through her head. She had not only gained a father but was about to learn more about her stepdad. Things were definitely looking up. "Thanks. How did you know it's my fave?" She drank from the mug.

"A hunch." He touched her arm. "Did Sam call you?"

"Yes. He told me everything."

"I'm sorry for my part in all of this. I've learned so much since Leah's death." He took a sip of his coffee. "God is teaching me a valuable lesson."

"And what's that?"

"I need to rely on Him more."

Did she? Could she trust Him with her life?

"Tell me about Rose." She took another sip, savoring the pumpkin flavor on her tongue.

His eyes lit up. "She was everything to me. I realize now that I took her for granted. Hard lesson."

Something passed through his eyes, but she didn't catch it in time to name it. Regret?

"She was an amazing woman and I miss her very much."

Madison's cell chimed with a text. Tucker. "Sorry,

I need to check this. Tucker and I are still investigating." She read his words.

Have proof Levine is Cicada. Be careful. Spotted in your area.

She stiffened.

"You okay?"

She shoved the phone aside. "I will be once we catch this guy."

"You will. Tucker is good at what he does." He placed his hand on top of hers. "He loves you, you know."

She snatched her hand back. "How would you know that?"

"He told me. Well, not in so many words, but his expression did."

Could that be true? If so, why did he pull away? Why—

Her vision blurred. The room spun.

She grasped the sides of the table.

"What's wrong? You okay?"

"I don't feel so good." She stumbled to her feet. "I need to go."

He jumped up. "Wait. Let me take you to a hospital."

"I don't—"

Her vision blurred again, and she glanced at Emerson.

The smirk on his face etched in her brain as her legs weakened.

Levine wasn't Cicada. An understanding slammed her in the gut.

Her stepfather hadn't changed.

Now she would die for trusting him.

God, save—

Darkness plunged her into the abyss before she finished her plea.

Tucker hung up after speaking with Jenkins and sat back, crossing his arms. He finally had proof of Levine's lies, but he still surmised danger lingered. What had he missed? Jenkins tracked Levine to the downtown area, close to where Madi was meeting with Emerson. Jenkins told Tucker to stay put. He'd handle everything, so why did Tucker's stomach feel like he swallowed concrete?

He texted Madi to check on her, but no response.

Kneading the muscles in his neck, he glanced at the time on his laptop—8:00 p.m. *Come on, Rob.* Tucker needed a reply on the note Leah had hidden. She wouldn't have done that if it wasn't something of vital importance.

Something he guessed would seal the case and end this madness.

His laptop dinged, announcing an email. Tucker leaned closer.

Finally.

He double clicked Rob's message and read.

Cracked the code after determining the algorithm. I'm attaching the file with the words of the message highlighted within the gibberish. You owe me big time. Stay safe, Rob.

Tucker opened the document.

Morvecet still making Dolumhart money. Haven't stopped production. Will take care of BC and eliminate other problem.

What? Obviously, a note from Levine. BC must be Brechin Cross, but who was the message intended for?

Had Leah deciphered the email and that was why she hid it where she knew her sister would find it?

The date was marked the day before Leah's accident.

He huffed out a breath and sat back. Something still niggled his brain.

Another ding sounded and he glanced at the email. Their forensic unit getting back to him on the video.

He opened it.

Cleaned this up for you.

Tucker double clicked the .mov file and watched the video again, halting at one voice.

"Don't you threaten me. Remember who's in charge here."

Tucker bolted out of his chair. He'd recognize that voice anywhere.

Emerson Peters.

And Madi was with him right now.

He grabbed his cell phone and punched in her number, racing out of the building. "Madi, pick up."

No answer.

Had he gotten to her?

Tucker googled the café's number and called.

"Border Junction Café. How may I help you?"

"This is Constable Tucker Reed. Do you know Madison Steele?"

"Yes."

"Is she at your café? I just tried calling her number."

"Oh, that's her phone. We wondered who left it behind."

Tucker unlocked his vehicle and jumped in. "She was with Emerson Peters. Is he there?"

"No, she fainted, so he said he would take her to the hospital."

Tucker hit the steering wheel, terror creeping into every inch of him. "How long ago?"

"An hour or so."

Tucker clicked off. How could he have been so stupid? Had Emerson been using him all along?

Some cop Tucker turned out to be.

Another mistake that may cost Madi her life.

Think, Tucker, think. Where would Emerson take her?

He ruled out his condo in town. Not private enough. Wait—

Didn't Sam say he worked on the Peterses' ranch? Where was that?

Tucker punched in Sam's number.

"Superintendent Sam Watson."

"Tucker here. Do you know if Emerson still owns the ranch you worked on years ago?"

"Last time I drove by, it was abandoned. Why?"

"He's Cicada. Has Madi. Tell me where the ranch is." Tucker realized he jumbled his words, but he didn't care. He was running out of time.

"Twenty minutes north of St. Stephen." He named the highway and markers to look for. "I'll meet you there."

"No. I'll have Hyatt assemble a team. It's too dangerous."

"I'm trained and she's my daughter. I just found her. You can't expect me to stay out of it now." He clicked off.

Tucker started the vehicle and pulled out of the detachment's parking lot. He hit the Bluetooth and brought Hyatt up to speed, requesting backup and the necessary equipment at the ranch.

Tucker raced through the small town with one thought on his mind.

Save his forever love.

Huntington's or not, he needed Madi in his life.

Crickets chirped, luring Madison awake. She blinked her eyes open, trying to sit and clear her foggy brain. Where was she? What happened?

Emerson.

He had drugged her.

He'd tied her hands to a wooden beam. She needed to get out of here. Wherever *here* was. The room smelled of faint manure, but the darkness prevented her from seeing anything else. She wiggled her fingers in an attempt to loosen the ropes.

Lord, please have Tucker find me.

Would God listen to her after everything she'd done?

A door creaked open and a light beamed into the building, revealing her surroundings.

Emerson held her in a barn.

He stepped inside, his face distorted into evil. Any kindness she'd seen earlier vanished. He held a rifle in one hand and a lantern in the other.

"Why? Why, Emerson?"

"I need to rule this province and the only way to do that is with money. A lot of money."

"You developed drugs that kill people."

He tsked, waggling his finger. "No, not me. Dolumhart. I just had them wrapped around my pinkie."

"Did you have Leah killed?"

His eyes narrowed. "No! He betrayed me and tried to take over my business."

"Daniel Levine?"

"Yes, but he's paid the price." He raised the light to reveal the corner of the barn.

Daniel Levine lay slumped against a hay bale, gunshot to the head.

Madison stilled at the sight. Emerson Peters was pure evil and was going to kill her too.

She needed to keep him talking so Tucker could find her. "Why did you push Tucker to investigate when you knew he might find out about you?"

Emerson threw his head back and laughed. "That idiot. He makes too many mistakes. I knew from the moment I met him I would enlist him to help me. Besides, I had to find out who betrayed me and killed Leah." He paused and looked toward the VP. "Once Leah told me her findings of a cover-up at Dolumhart, I demanded Daniel use Andy to get rid of the files. What he didn't realize was I also hired a hacker to get me into both Leah's and *his* records. I didn't trust the man. He was just too eager to please. I found out Levine double-crossed me by skimming off the profits. My hacker also found evidence of Leah's hit buried deep inside his files and I knew then Daniel had caused her accident. I needed Tucker to prove it without raising suspicion."

Unbelievable. Madison twisted her bound hands. She had to escape. "So you continued to work with

Daniel anyway to keep producing the drug even though Leah uncovered the results?"

"My daughter was too smart. I miss her." He exhaled loudly. "I needed Daniel on the inside. However, my campaign will prevail. I have enough money now to win." He eyed the body. "He was no longer of use to me and had to pay for Leah's death."

"Why tell Sam to confess to being my dad?"

"To get any scent off my trail. I knew my action would solidify my intentions. Get you on my good side and to trust me, so I could get closer to you. Of course, saving your life also helped. That was an unexpected gift." He chuckled. "I'm good at what I do."

"What? Deceiving everyone?" Yes, she gave it to him. He *was* good. "Was it you texting me all those threatening messages? How did you get my number?"

He sneered. "My black-hat hackers were able to get into your records and help me send them without you even realizing it was me. My goons also tried to nab you, but that constable intervened. Can't find good help these days. Had to do it myself."

His face contorted into a repulsive sneer.

Madison cringed. How had she ever thought he was handsome?

"How did you distribute it?" She needed to understand more and give Tucker time.

"That you haven't figured out yet."

"So what, you're going to kill me?"

He snickered. "Not me."

"I am."

Charlotte stepped from the shadows into the lantern's glow.

Madison recoiled, scrambling back against the beam.

"That's right, Madison, dear. I sold the drugs right from my ambulance."

"It was you who switched the drugs and killed Dolly, wasn't it?"

"Smart girl. Dolly figured it out, so when she fainted and they dispatched us to Susan's salon, I used the moment to eliminate a loose end. I'd already made the switch and was just waiting for the opportune time. Teddy administering it was an added bonus."

"Why are you helping Emerson? Aren't you trained to save people, not kill them?"

"I needed the money. You see, Emerson here found out about my gambling habit when I worked for him at his campaign."

Emerson set the rifle down and grabbed a pitchfork. "That's right. I offered her money for her help." He stepped closer.

Was he going to ram the fork into Madison?

She closed her eyes and waited for the pain.

A thud sounded and she opened her eyes again.

He'd stabbed it in the hay next to her. "Tucker

won't find you. I will see to that. I've always hated you. You're nothing more than an illegitimate piece of trash!"

Terror jabbed Madison in the chest, freezing her limbs. She fought for breaths as trepidation clawed each inhale away. How could he have such a deep hatred toward the stepdaughter he barely knew?

He turned to Charlotte. "It's time. Do it."

Emerson untied Madison from the pole and hauled her up.

She squirmed and tried to flee, but Charlotte pulled out a knife and grabbed Madison's arm. "Nice try. Let's go."

"Why do you want to kill me, Charlotte?"

"Because *he* loves you, not *me*."

Tucker?

Charlotte pushed her out of the barn and into the night under the darkened skies. "I've always hated you."

The crickets chirped louder and Madison checked the surroundings. They were in the middle of nowhere.

"This way," Charlotte said, nudging her behind a structure.

God, save me.

Charlotte stopped in front of a stone well. "Don't worry, there's no water left in there, but this is where you die. Just remember something. I will console Tucker when he finds you dead." She thrust the knife into Madison's stomach and pushed her into the well.

Madison's head struck the stone wall on the way down, plunging her into darkness.

Tucker approached the ranch with the team at his flank and Sam behind him. They had gathered at the property's edge, formulating a plan to rescue Madi. Jenkins would circle around back with his team, and Tucker, Hyatt and Sam would storm the front door. They reached the driveway and Tucker raised his hand in a stop signal.

"Goggles on," Tucker whispered. He pressed his radio button. "Jenkins, you ready?"

"Affirmative."

"On my signal." He gestured his team to stay low and position themselves by the trees surrounding the ranch's veranda.

Someone skulked in the house.

It was time. "Breach! Now!"

Tucker stood aside and let his fellow officers break down the front door with their battering ram. He raised his weapon and rushed forward. "Police! Stand down, Emerson."

A crash from the rear told Tucker Jenkins had also entered the ranch.

"You're surrounded," Tucker yelled. "Where is Madi?"

A wicked laugh sounded from behind the kitchen

partition, resonating throughout the lower level. "Somewhere you'll never find her."

Tucker clenched his entire body as panic threatened to overcome him. "Give yourself up, Emerson."

"You have no evidence, Tucker."

"That's where you're wrong. Your daughter was smart and hid it for us to find. You're done, Cicada."

"So, you figured it out, huh?"

"Why Cicada?"

"Have you never heard the background of the summer bug? It lies in the ground for years before surfacing to the world, and their song pierces in the hot months." He snickered. "I'm about to emerge to the world as the next premier. Loud and mighty."

Tucker shook his head. "Only you would name yourself after a bug that dies weeks after facing the world."

Sam inched to Tucker's right, heading through a side door.

The CBSA superintendent knew the ranch better than them, and Tucker trusted the man's instincts. Tucker prayed for God's intervention in the situation. He didn't want anyone to die, not even Cicada. He needed to pay for what he'd done.

"How did you stay ahead of us in the investigation?"

Emerson snorted. "Like I told your dear *Madi*, well-placed individuals and black-hat hackers.

You'd be surprised what money can buy. I bribed a janitor to steal Leah's flash drive. Plus, my men followed you wherever you went and you didn't even know it. What kind of a cop are you? Obviously, not a good one."

Tucker cringed at the man's hurtful words but let them go and held his weapon higher. "Emerson, surrender. You didn't kill Leah and don't have blood on your hands. Yet."

"Don't be so sure."

No, Lord! Please help Madi not to be dead.

"Maybe a judge will go easy on you." Tucker doubted it.

"On a crooked politician? Hardly, Tucker." He popped his head up, rifle in hand. "And here I told Madison you were an idiot."

Tucker flinched, realization pelting his mind that this man had lied to him ever since they'd met. *How could you be so stupid?*

"Emerson, you have nowhere to run."

"You're too late. She's dead."

No! Wouldn't he know if she had died? Feel it? Tucker raised his machine gun higher. "I don't believe you. Drop the weapon!"

"You first."

"No way. You need to pay for your sins."

"Have it your way." Emerson stepped from behind the counter and leveled the rifle at Tucker.

Sam lunged from the shadows, ramming his body into Emerson's.

They catapulted to the floor, entangled in a crocodile death roll.

The rifle shot across the floor and Tucker stepped on it to stop its trajectory. He rushed forward and leveled his weapon on Emerson. "You're done."

Emerson sneered. "You won't find her in time."

Tucker slammed the end of his rifle into Cicada's head, knocking him unconscious.

He helped Sam to his feet. "Good work."

"We need to find her."

The rest of the team rushed into the room.

Tucker waved his hands. "Spread out. Search the property. She has to be here somewhere."

Hyatt secured Emerson. "You go—I'll watch him."

Tucker bolted into the night in search of his love.

Madison opened her eyes to pitch-blackness, cold air chilling her to the bone. She was going to die. Her worst fears were coming true. However, suddenly it wasn't death that scared her any longer.

It was the fact that she never got to tell Tucker how she really felt.

She had never stopped loving him.

And now it was too late.

And God? Would He forgive her after everything she'd done running away from Him? Where was He? Bren's words returned.

You just need to know where to look.

Was God with her in the well? Right now? Could she trust Him with all the unknown?

Hope.

The word raced into her mind. She needed to place her trust and hope back into the One she now realized had never left her, even during everything. Pain stabbed her stomach where Charlotte's blade had pierced, but she knew it wasn't the end. With God, the unknown shouldn't be feared. There was hope in the Eternal. Madison peered up through the well as a cloud parted in the sky, twinkling lights emerging.

Just like her heart.

God, I know I haven't lived for You all these years, but I surrender. I'm sorry. I give my life back to You. Whatever is left of it. Take it. I'm yours. Forever and always.

Peace washed over her, even in her chilled tomb. Yes, God had stopped the traffic for her all those years ago when she'd lost control of her bike and she didn't know if He would stop her death now, but she was ready. Ready to face the unknown. She had hope she'd see the loved ones gone on before her.

And that intensified the peace coursing through her veins.

Tucker, I'm sorry.

A muffled yell stilled her. What was that?

"Madi! Where are you?"

Tucker?

God intervened. Just like all those years ago.

"I'm down here." Her voice cracked, the sound stopping before it could reach Tucker's ears. She had to get higher.

Mustering all the strength and courage her injured body could find, she stood and reached for indentations in the rock formation. Her fingers clasped onto a stone and she climbed.

High.

Higher.

"Tucker! I'm down here!"

Pounding footsteps approached and a light shone in the well, blinding her.

"Madi! You're alive." He shouted an order to someone behind him. "We'll get you out. Hold on."

Moments later, a rope fell in beside her. "Tucker, Charlotte stabbed me in the stomach."

"What? You okay?"

"Weak, but God's given me strength to fight."

"Wrap the rope under your armpits," Tucker said. "We'll pull you up slowly."

She obeyed. They hoisted her to the surface.

Tucker gently wrapped his arms under hers and tugged her from the well.

She fell into his embrace, her limbs turning to jelly and sobs catching in her throat. "I'm sorry. I'm sorry."

"For what? I was the one who pushed you to see Emerson. I'm to blame."

"No, it's not your fault. Where is he?"

"Your dad tackled him. Hyatt has him in custody."

"Sam is here?"

"Who do you think helped find this place?"

Of course. She was conceived at the ranch and now almost died here. How ironic. She grabbed her stomach, the pain from her wound intensifying. How much blood had she lost? Would an ambulance get there in time? *Tell him. Before it's too late.* "Tucker, I need to tell you the truth."

He placed a finger on her lips. "Not now."

"No. I need to tell you why I've been distant and why I really broke up with you." She paused. "After I moved to Quebec, I met a man named Lucas. We got engaged and then the day of our wedding, he died from a heart attack."

"What?"

"That's why I moved back to New Brunswick. I needed to distance myself from the pain." She harrumphed. "I now see I did the same thing when I broke up with you. I ran away."

"I'm so sorry you had to go through that." Tucker squeezed her harder.

She winced.

He pulled back. "I'm sorry."

Madison gulped; a question gnawed through her brain. "Where's Charlotte?"

"She must have fled. We didn't see anyone else on the grounds."

"You didn't look very hard, handsome." Charlotte stepped from behind the well's shadows, gun at her side. "Nice little reunion, but now you will both pay for interfering."

"Why, Charlotte?" Tucker asked, shifting his body in front of Madison's.

"Don't you get it? Because you never loved me." She raised her sidearm. "I won't use a knife this time. Obviously, I picked the wrong weapon earlier. Now you both die."

A shot rang out and Charlotte dropped.

Madison yelled and turned.

Sam stood with his gun in hand.

Madison stood on shaky legs, clutching her stomach, and stumbled into her father's arms. "You saved us."

"I just found you. I wasn't going to lose you too." He cried in her embrace.

Jenkins and the team rushed to the scene. "Paramedics are en route." He eyed Charlotte's body. "Real paramedics."

Sam released Madison. "Go with Tucker. We've got this."

Tucker helped Madison over to the front porch.

She sat and leaned her head on his shoulder. "Okay, now for the truth. The real reason I broke up with you that day."

"You don't have to."

"I want you back in my life, so I need to confess and I pray you will forgive me." She paused and gathered strength. "I had just found out about being adopted and then my parents were killed. I blamed God, so I joined a bunch of kids one night. We went around to a half a dozen churches and created havoc. We painted graffiti on their buildings, tore down crosses. You name it, we did it. No violence though. Just childish defacing of property." She sat up, turning her face to his. "I had hated that you became a Christian and I knew you'd never forgive me for what I'd done."

"That's why you broke up with me?"

She nodded.

He rubbed her chin with his thumb. "I forgive you even though it's not me you need to ask forgiveness from."

"I will make it up to those churches. I surrendered to God. In the well."

He pulled her back into his arms. "I'm so glad." He sighed in her ear and released her. "I need to confess something too and you might change your mind about me. But my mother is right. I need to give you the choice."

"What are you talking about?"

"You remember my father left years ago?"

"Yes."

"He left because he had Huntington's disease and didn't want his family to watch him deteriorate." He paused.

"And you think you might have inherited it?"

He nodded.

She cupped his chin in her hands. "I choose you,

Tucker. We'll face it together." A cricket chirped, bringing happiness instead of fear. "I love you."

A tear spilled down her cheek.

He wiped it away. "I never stopped loving you, my sweet Madi." He inched closer, eyeing her lips.

Madi. She now loved how it rolled off his tongue. She closed her eyes and his lips met hers in a tender, forever kiss.

She'd done it. She conquered her fears and found her love—to infinity and beyond.

EPILOGUE

A year later—Thanksgiving Day

Madison walked to the Celtic Cross and placed a fall wreath beside a bush. A hummingbird hovered for a split second before fluttering away and reminding Madison of how quickly life can change. Her fear of death and the unknown had kept her in a vise grip for too long, but the night she almost died a year ago gave her back hope. Hope in God. Hope in her forever love. Hope for when the unknown crept back into her life. She could handle it now with Christ.

She fingered the cross pendant around her neck and remembered her sister's saying—to infinity and beyond. Their sisterly love would never die, and one day they'd be reunited.

Madison stood and let the breeze flow through her long hair. The water stilled from yesterday's storm, mirroring their surroundings. She glanced over at the bench where Tucker waited. Ever since that night at Emerson's ranch, they'd grown closer. He had gotten tested and found out he didn't have the Huntington's gene, but even if he did, she knew she would have stuck by his side. His mother had fully recovered. The antidote was reproduced and given to other victims. All Morvecet was destroyed. The courts found Emerson guilty on all charges, including the murder of Daniel Levine. He was now in prison.

Daniel had emailed Jenkins earlier that day, confessing to everything. He knew Emerson was on his tail and would kill him. The situation saddened Madison. She never knew if Leah had known about her father, but in a way she hoped she hadn't. For her sake.

Sam, Madison's biological father, had barely let her out of his sight. They'd become close, and he even started dating Brenda. Madison smiled at the thought of her sweet housekeeper finding genuine love after so many years. The woman cooked a full Thanksgiving feast which waited for them at Madison's home.

She stood and made her way back over to Tucker. "Thank you for coming with me." She sat and leaned her head on his, wrapping her arms around him. "I love it here."

"Anything for you." He squirmed out of her embrace and squatted in front of her, holding a box.

He opened it.

A diamond sparkled in the sunlight.

She gasped.

He removed the solitaire and held it out. "I love you, Madi. Will you make me the happiest man on earth and be my wife?"

A tear formed and she jumped up. "Yes! Yes!"

Tucker put the ring on her finger and stood. He pulled her into his arms and twirled her around.

A thought emerged.

The high school sweethearts were now back together—always and forever.

* * * * *

*If you liked this story from Darlene L. Turner,
check out her previous
Love Inspired Suspense books:*

Border Breach
Abducted in Alaska

Available now from Love Inspired Suspense!

Find more great reads at www.LoveInspired.com

Dear Reader,

Thank you for reading Madison and Tucker's novel. I enjoyed setting it in my hometown province of New Brunswick. This is a story about sisterly love and friendship. Of course, I had to write my sister in there somewhere and because she's a hair stylist, I put Susan's salon in the downtown core. I also crafted Madison's fictitious backstory loosely after my sweet mother-in-law, Bev, who was adopted and found her sister sixty-three years after separation.

I wrote this book during the tough year our world faced living in the unknown. Madison and Tucker are stuck in fear but eventually find hope. Hope in the unknown and hope in knowing God is in control and with us—no matter the circumstances. We just need to know where to look.

I'd love to hear from you. You can contact me through my website www.darlenelturner.com and also sign up for Darlene's Diary newsletter to receive exclusive subscriber giveaways.

God bless,
Darlene L. Turner